WILLHEIM BRANDT

Cameo Trail Series
Book 1

JANA DAHMEN

Publishing Coordinator – Sharon Kizziah-Holmes
Cover Artist – Jana Dahmen

Paperback-Press
an imprint of A & S Publishing
Paperback Press, LLC
Springfield, Missouri

ISBN -13: 978-1-964559-41-4

Acknowledgments

My husband Marv Dahmen allows the time I need to be obsessed with my writing. It takes hours, and he is very patient and understanding. My man is a wonderful husband!

My Sister-Friend, Cindy Harrold, in Joplin, Missouri gives me so much encouragement. She listens to me when I'm up and when I'm down. I love her so much!

Gary Schubert in Sweetwater, Texas is my go-to cowboy who answers my questions about horses and Nolan County whenever I get stuck.

Sharon Kizziah-Holmes is my mentor. I'm proud to call her a friend and thankful for all she does to make my books come to life. You couldn't ask for a better publishing company than Paperback Press.

Prologue

Willheim Brandt was just another cowboy carving out a life for himself in the west like so many other young men after 1850 during the western expansion. His German parents and those before them were farmers. They had amassed a large amount of farmland and open range near Sweetwater, Texas through hard work and government options offered to settle the land.

He was well-versed in the tasks of farming, but he wanted to see and experience other things before he was tied down to the land. Will, quite the greenhorn when he left home, had no idea what all he would witness before he was ready to reclaim his roots.

~Imagine just this one excerpt recorded between the pages of this book describing an unforgettable experience Willhelm Brandt lived through. Driving herds of longhorns across the prairie was not for the faint hearted. Many men succumbed to the perils and nature's harsh elements along the trails.

As the storm conditions continued to worsen, every steer in the herd grew increasingly wilder and glassier eyed, and the animals churned more nervously. As the tension levels ratcheted, the heads of the cattle tipped upward and were held higher in anticipation of the pending danger. All available hands were dispersed to help keep the animals as calm as possible and bunched together in a compact group.

As anxiety increased, so did the stressful noises emanating from deep within their throats, followed by blows of air expelling through their nostrils. The humid air grew thicker minute by minute, and the wind picked up. At this point anything, the jangle of a single jingle bob dangling from a spur, one word spoken above a whisper, a cough, the wrinkling of the smallest paper, or the striking of a match, could set the whole herd into flight all at once.

A single streak of lightning hit much too closely ripping down from the sky. The visual flash was instantaneously followed by a deafening, mighty loud crack of thunder. The earth immediately shook under the pounding of the longhorns' hooves much like an earthquake. The powerful tremors jarred every living creature all the way up to the crowns of their heads and down along the spines of their backs.

The already agitated herd took off in one body as if washed out to sea riding an ocean wave. The herd was sent away in one swift motion with the force of an iron locomotive. There was no stopping the surge of tons and tons of panicked beef cattle already dancing on their hooves. The race was on, and God help the cowboys who tried to control the longhorns!

Cowboys worked as teams and did their best to slowdown the charging animals. Some riders headed for the front of the herd. The cowboys fired guns above their heads in an effort to turn the steers and keep the herd from scattering in all different directions.

The men whooped, hollered, and pushed themselves and the horses beyond their limits. Coiled lariats were waved frantically in the air to redirect the frightened, massive force into a circle formation moving counterclockwise. All prayed the longhorns would soon run out of steam and come to a stop.

All the while, lightning and thunder continued along with the high wind, rain, and pelting hail coming down in stinging and confusing assaults. These torturing blows of nature hit men and animals equally without mercy. The storm unloaded every element it had down upon men and beasts alike. This onslaught combined with the darkened sky cut visibility to nearly nothing, and verbal communication was impossible.

During the height of this frenzy Eddy Flores, the trail boss, was knocked from his saddle. A five-foot tall, twelve-hundred-pound steer broadsided Eddy's gelding! The man was knocked off its back.

Through sporadic flashes of lightning, Willheim Brandt, the young cowboy, looked on in shock and horror as he witnessed all of this happen!

~A Little History about the Historic Cattle Drives~

During the second half of the 19th century, after the Civil War, many soldiers came home to find little to nothing of the lives they had left behind. They were desperate to find ways to earn wages.

With five to six million unclaimed and feral, longhorns wandering loose on the prairies, the government made them available for the taking. The stray cattle were free to whomever had the pluckiness and grit to round them up. Even if they wore a brand, anyone could legally claim the longhorns and rebrand them.

Men willing and able to do the work seized this opportunity to generate incomes. Many former soldiers from the north and the south seized the chance and met the dangerous job head-on. The whole United States suddenly had an insatiable appetite for beef. In the east, there were especially deep pockets willing to pay for it.

Two magic words of the western expansion era were free and plentiful. Indeed, the longhorns were both of these things. When it came to making money off of the animals, however, nothing came easily. Much back-breaking work and many long hours were in store for the men before any money would cross hands.

The ornery strays had to be caught, and the bulls then had to be castrated. All of the longhorns needed a brand or a rebranding. These undertakings were all hard and dangerous. Then, they had to be driven far to the locations where buyers waited to pay as much as forty dollars a head and ship them off to the hungry consumers in the east.

Herding longhorns for hundreds of miles was a monumental task, and again, the endeavor was risky. Only a certain type of men was willing or courageous enough to tackle a trail drive. It took vision, grit, and a whole lot of manpower to get such an ambitious job done. These people became known as ranchers, cowboys, and cattle drovers.

This type of work drew both men and boys because of financial desperation, a lust for adventure, or a way to evade personal responsibilities or the law. The lure of the trails, the comradery among men, and the pull of insatiable wanderlust was powerful. Any man tough enough to survive the wilds, head 'em up, and move those dogies out deserved bragging rights!

Make no mistake, this was a dicey commitment. The herculean challenges of crossing the tall grass plains on horseback were rife with rustlers, natives, storms, stampedes, accidents, deep rivers, and scant watering holes. The grueling days spent in a hard, leather saddle either proved a man's worth or broke him down.

The skittish, undomesticated animals could average horn spans of up to eight feet. One formidable steer called Buckle Head in Rocksprings, Texas, was recorded to have a horn span measuring eleven feet, one and one-eighth inch from tip-to-tip. Another impressive steer's span from Alabama measured ten feet, seven and four-tenths inches. Poncho was this big fellow's name. Both were written down in history.

Longhorns, by nature, were notoriously ill-tempered. Rounding strays up from bramble filled terrains and keeping hundreds of the unruly critters going in the same direction for days on end were difficult and dirty jobs at best. Mix in the changeability of weather conditions and the journeys could be downright deadly. At one time, cowhands pushed thousands of longhorns in huge herds to reach markets.

It has been said the cowboys feared the dangers of a stampede above all other perils on the trail.

CHAPTER 1

THE SWEET, SWEET WATER OF TEXAS

Christmas 1878

The man, Willheim Brandt, is a seasoned cowboy on his way back home for Christmas. He had just kicked loose dirt over the remains of what he hoped would be his last campfire for a long spell. He is weary of moving around from place to place untethered like tumbleweed.

After years of roaming, following huge herds of tetchy longhorns and working on other men's spreads to fill their pockets, he isn't looking for any more new adventures. He is fairly certain he's seen every part of the elephant there is to see, firsthand and up close.

His mind is made up to return home to Sweetwater and stay put for good this time. His own land is sitting there just waiting for him to figure out what he wants to do with it. The itch to stay put and do something meaningful has finally hit him. Several worthy ideas are bouncing around in his head.

With the sole of his worn boot, he makes sure to rub

every single, glowing ember down to dust. He pours what little leftover coffee there is on the exact place his campfire had burned courageously last night. He'd fed this fire and a thousand others like it through too many nights to count. This time felt special though. His home sweet home is just over the horizon.

Yesterday's aroma and popping of the native mesquite wood burning had been comforting. Heat from the spirit of the flames warmed him to his bones, and the beautiful sparkles rose upward high into the air where they died and disappeared. The fire had given its energy to cook his grub with the faint mesquite flavor he always loved to taste. While wild critters palavered back and forth to each other on and off during the night, it warned them to stay back in the darkness away from the glow.

As usual, he and his dogs had awoken before daylight. Sunrise followed on the coat tails of the crisp, cold air of dawn. The magical sight of hoarfrost made the world around him look like an inviting fairyland.

It was late December and tonight would be Christmas Eve-Eve. He would celebrate at home with a big meal, tall tales, and lots of laughter with family. Officially, Christmas Eve was tomorrow night. The tree would be decorated, stockings hung, and a big pot of something good to eat would simmer on the stove. He is headed to the Brandt homestead, the place of his birth. This is the season best spent with family.

This morning he'd pulled the dwindling chunk of salted side meat wrapped in cheesecloth from his saddle bag. Using his hunting knife, he had cut thick rashers of bacon from it until it was all gone. These strips of meat were cooked over the heat of his dying fire. The pieces curled, and grease sputtered and spit in the skillet.

The smell alone was mouthwatering. Nothing went to waste on the trail from the smells, to the rich tastes, and to the scraps tossed to his dogs. Even the hot rendered grease was used for sopping dry, stale biscuits from his grub sack. The hard, crusty bread greedily soaked up every drop of fat. The grease softened them up right fine and added flavor.

Victuals like these are typical fare for a cowboy traveling the long, lonely trails. His three brush dogs were used to receiving a share and nervously whined to be noticed. With his belly full and body well-rested, Will is comfortable and ready to head out. He loves the desolation of the West Texas range with its wide-open spaces.

New pilgrims stopping here hadn't bargained for such prolonged spells of isolation, and the harsh climate is much more severe than they had imagined. Mostly unprepared, the settlers sheltered in primitive dugouts, sod houses, and crude lean-tos. They survived as best they could, like fish out of water.

The extreme winters, as well as the burning summers, are punishing and unforgiving. The tall grass prairie doesn't take kindly to being broken by plows and reluctantly yields to domestic demands. The first crops are grown only from blood, sweat, and tears. The newcomers didn't bargain on this many hardships just to stay alive so far from neighbors and civilized services.

Willheim Brandt was born of strong, German stock, and his people had done fine in this land. They survived and held onto many of the traditions from the old country. Every Christmas, the Brandts yearned to reunite the whole family together around one hearth to celebrate the holy birth of Christ. They rejoiced remembering His gift to all mankind.

This is a coveted time for the Brandts and as many as possible always make it home for Christmas each year. There is strength together holding tightly to shared memories of the past.

Will had started the annual trip home a little earlier than usual this year because he had reached a crossroads in his life. He needs time to think and settle on the direction he wants to go. What did he want his future to look like? These are heavy, personal ponderings, and choices must be considered before he makes decisions. Where does he want to be and what does he need to have when he gets there?

After much soul searching, he has decided it is time for him to build a house on his waiting land. Then he'll court a good, decent woman, marry, and start his own family. It seems simple enough to him, but it also means he has some necessary changes to make.

Before he can even start, he knows his morally sketchy involvement with Elizabeth Hartley has to come to an end. A cowardly voice in his head is begging him to avoid unpleasantness, ignore the existence of the girl, and quietly disappear without explanation. The grown man in his head speaks louder and demands him to meet his mistakes head on. Go see her one last time to bury the history of their dalliances and to say he's sorry.

He dreads the looming encounter as much as having a tooth pulled, but the more mature voice of his conscience wins the duel. He has to go talk to her today before reaching Papa's house. A man has to do what a man has to do in order to live with himself. The time has come to cowboy up and face the music so he can let go of the past!

Will has the hope all the brothers and his little maverick sister, Kat, will be able to make it home this year. His oldest sister, Meta Anna, her husband, Nick, and their three children lived in Papa's house with him. His sister, Savanah, her husband, Ely, and their children live in back of Sweetwater's general store. Ely's father had built it from the ground up, and his only son inherited it when the man died.

Will had been completely caught off guard last December when he'd ridden in and found his Mama, Matilda, had passed away. He arrived home to find his mother had been laid to rest in the red dirt right by the place Papa will also be buried someday. She'd died only a couple of weeks earlier, and her absence had hit him hard.

Will had seen too much death on the trail and learned never to take a day on this good earth for granted. Death had to be taken in stride as the natural order of things. The days of a person's life on earth are numbered. Sickness and accidents can happen quickly, and the last breath can go just as fast as the first breath of life can come.

In the natural order of things, Meta Anna had quietly slipped into his mother's role in Papa's house. She and her family took care of him and kept the home fires burning. Nick had already been managing the family farm for a while already. He has no doubt his sister at this very moment is cooking up a storm in anticipation of all her brothers' and sisters' arrivals.

Nick was used to the whole kith and kin swooping down on the old homestead as well. They'd all make merry together for a week, a month, or more, depending on how much time each can stay. Will knows his papa is watching the road anxiously this time of year for the dust trails announcing another child returning home.

It set Will to thinking how much he'd grown in body and confidence since the day he left home the first time. He'd only been a green kid, a young boy from Sweetwater, with nothing but his brothers' colorful tales of cowboy life to stoke his grandiose dreams.

His first step to independence was the hardest. It took a lot of gumption for a skinny farm boy to traipse out into the mystery of the world to face it by himself. For sure, he was frightened to leave the totally safe and predictable farm he knew, but he was too curious not to step out and discover whatever was waiting out there for him.

The romanticized idea of cowboys roaming freely and following the trails of the Texas Longhorns eventually became too much for him to ignore. Driving a large herd of cattle northward or eastward to be sold and slaughtered for beef was a fun idea. Being paid to do it was a bonus. Will fully intended to ride a strong horse behind longhorns and sleep out under the stars like a king!

It turned out young Will had a knack for the life of a cowboy, and he thrived out on the endless prairies. He has several successful years under his belt now as a successful herdsman, but he is restless again and yearns for something more. It is time to take a chance again.

There are giant changes barreling across the land on the heels of heavy, iron wheels. This powerful progress in transportation has hit everyday life with a force too fast to be held back. Rail is being laid by the mile, right through rock mountains and other impassable terrains. Steam engine trains are taking the place of the stagecoaches.

Old ways of life are on the cusp of being run over by new, improved, faster, and more profitable ways. He doesn't understand all of the unprecedented impacts these shifts may have on a frontier society. Definitely, nothing is going to stay the same for much longer.

The future of the cowboys with the fencing of the open frontier is causing friction. More and more barbed wire is being stretched by small homesteaders. Large ranchers are throwing in together and forming associations for the purpose of strong-arming the smaller landowners.

This turmoil is part of why he has decided not to look for a spring herd to drive up one of the well-established trails next season. The rules of the prairie are changing rapidly, and rising conflicts are unavoidable. There is talk of range wars, and Will isn't interested in riding into the middle of fighting.

Five years of working for a trail boss in both the spring and fall and pushing cows up the Goodnight-Loving Trail or one of the others was enough. Especially when he is a landowner himself and can work his own spread.

This spring will be the dawn of his twenty-third birthday, and he has a hankering to settle down on his share of Papa's land. His heart wasn't in farming though. Turning sod doesn't suit him. His brother-in-law, Nick, is a farmer and manages Papa's farming operation which benefits all of them. Will is glad of it, because with his experience of working on big spreads, he is determined to raise horses. He'll probably run a few cattle eventually too.

He is riding his stout, black gelding, named Rope Tail, and trailing three others on this trip. Two were easily carrying everything he owned. One of the horses, a small, two-colored mare, will be a gift for Nick. It is a way of saying thanks for having the crowd descend upon his peaceful home and for looking after Papa.

A token of appreciation for Nick's hospitality is in order, Nickolas can always use another good horse. This mare possesses a fine, gentle heart and will be easy handling for his wife and growing family.

Most of the old cowboys didn't set much store in a horse of more than one color. It was thought to be a sign of inbreeding, and the old timers still swore the animal to be slower of mind and body. Will was skeptical of their beliefs, because he'd seen a number of one-colored horses with dull heads as well as bad temperaments.

The manner of this particular mare stole his heart from the beginning with her doe-like eyes, soft muzzle, and sweet as sugar disposition. She has a habit of giving him a soft nudge in the back if given a chance. The gesture tickles Will, and he enjoys her playfulness.

He is fond of this affectionate horse. Her tender spirit will fit right well on the farm with all the nieces and nephews to ride and pet her. She deserves more than to be used hard for pushing cattle all day and being cussed by rude men.

Long ago, when he joined his first cattle drive, he learned to respect the opinions of the older cowpokes with grizzled faces and scars to back up their stories. Will soaked up their recollections as pure, prairie gospel. The elder hands had witnessed a thing or two over the years and were a wealth of information. They were willing to share their experiences, and all agreed on one basic thing, the surer the mount the safer the rider. A man in trouble with a savvy, dependable horse between his legs has less chance of losing a limb or his life.

A cowboy always had to stay alert and be prepared for the unexpected. It wasn't if he'd find himself in a tight spot but when he'd find himself in trouble. Sooner or later, every cowboy gets caught between a rock and a hard place in a split second. He witnessed times cowboys had been protected from injury because of the sureness of the horse he was riding. The soundness of a working horse was nothing to be taken for granted.

Picking a good horse to ride was of major importance when facing longhorns on the open range. Impulsiveness had no place when building your string. Will never forgot the lesson he'd learned the hard way on his first drive. He'd been a lad with only a puppy dog eagerness back then, and he'd had a lot to learn.

CHAPTER 2

WILD NED THE LEGEND!

The moment young Will stepped foot into the realm of Eddy Flores, he sensed he had entered a separate world. Nothing had prepared him for the slam of culture shock. He was swallowed up into a people made up of cowboys in every size, color, and age. He walked around in awe, unnoticed, and turning in every direction, taking it all in.

On his first day with Eddy Flores's outfit, a herd of green-broke mustangs arrived in a haze of dust driven up from the great Rio Grande by none other than Wild Ned Mason himself and his mesteñeros!

The boy had never heard of a Wild Ned Mason before, but it was clear from the beginning, every man admired him as an authority on horses. The burly, giant of a man rode a black horse flanked by three scruffy-looking dogs.

Young Will was smart enough to hang back in the commotion, and he caught the drift these horses would make up the outfit's remuda. The herd of horses were only green, broken. The cowboys would choose from them to be their mounts for each day.

He was naturally an astute listener, an observer of details, and had a quick-minded nature. These attributes, along with knowing when to keep his mouth shut, had always served him well. He had many unfamiliar things to learn very quickly.

Willheim didn't miss the earnest eyes of the weathered cowboys as they studied the horseflesh and talked among themselves. Will took notice of the various opinions based on the evidence of each horse's stature. He listened intently and took note of which animals were favored most by the majority and of the horses most often ignored. He critically studied all of them in both classes.

He appreciated the scrutiny of the men as they identified strengths and weaknesses. Willheim soaked up their opinions of standards for determining good horse flesh. It was clear each man wanted the best horse under him on the days ahead.

Eventually, every cowboy was given a fair chance to select his own string of mounts one-by-one. The trail boss, Mr. Flores, had the privilege of choosing his entire string first since he'd spend more hours in the saddle than anyone. The men judged their leader's savvy by the ones he chose.

The boss may have felt the pressure of his reputation hanging in the balance, but it never showed on his face. He took time to pick a number of what he considered to be the best suited. Nods and murmurings from the gallery reflected respect.

After the boss's personal string was cut from the mix, the boys were left to cast lots to determine the order each cowboy would select one horse at a time. This lottery system ensured every vaquero had a fair chance at the remaining hundred head.

To his surprise, Will was given the same chance as the seasoned men. This both fed his ego and unnerved his bowels. He tried not to be obvious, but he made a short-stepped trip to the outhouse before his first turn.

Those who'd drawn slots ahead of him made their first selections, and all too soon, his name was called for a first turn. All eyes were pinned on the junior newcomer. He broke out in a sweat and prayed for God's help.

Using the very brief education from observing the others, he chose a big, dappled grey mare. He dared not breathe as he watched for signs from his mentors. The men gave him nods, grunts, and hard slaps of encouragement on his back. Will had passed the first test of many he'd endure in the next weeks.

He remembered how he had swelled with unearned pride in front of the smaller thirteen-year-old hired to work part time with the wrangler and the rest of his time as the cook's biscuit roller. He was also labeled the cook's mollie or little Mary.

The three titles were derogatory titles. They were meant to be patronizing but to be used without malice. Step-and-fetch-it-boy, kitchen hand, or designated dish washer would have been more accurate descriptions but none the less demeaning. The boy was allowed to use one of the unclaimed horses when he wasn't driving the wagon pulled by oxen or collecting firewood.

Will's first drive was relatively average in size with less than two thousand head of bad tempered, unpredictable, untamed, and stubborn Texas Longhorns headed for Dodge City, Kansas. It had been the only outfit offering to hire Will's inexperience. He had no idea how lucky he was to get the job.

It wasn't until years after he found out his adopted, black brother, Mateas Brown Brandt, had arranged for this position as a favor owed him by the trail boss, Eddy Flores. At the time, knowing would have stung his fragile ego, but now it spoke of brotherly love. Perspective has a way of changing with time.

Willheim Brandt, next to the youngest in the family, left for South Texas on a used-up plow horse. It was the only one his frugal German father would spare for yet one more boy's passage into adulthood. Will was beginning to understand how difficult it must have been for Papa to lose his last son to the call of the wild.

Martin and Matilda Brandt had borne or chosen to raise seven children. Willheim Berterm Brandt was the next to the youngest child with Katrina Marie being the baby of the family. These two were as close and mischievous as raccoon kits. They were definitely ring-tailed-tooters!

The first born and oldest child was Meta Anna who married Nickolas Austin and became Meta Anna Brandt Austin. Then, four boys arrived in rapid succession starting with Morgan Josiah Brandt, followed by Mateas Brown Brandt, a black orphan. He was raised as one of their own with exactly the same privileges.

The third boy before Willheim was Tavias Martin Brandt. Tavy and Will were more than simply brothers. They were the best of friends.

There were three girls. Savannah Grace Brandt, who was actually a cousin. She was a few months younger than Meta Anna. She'd been taken into the fold at eight to be raised as a daughter. Her parents were killed in a fire. She married a Sweetwater merchant named Ely Benton, making her name Savannah Grace Brandt Benton.

Every one of the Brandt children left the homestead except Meta and her husband, Nick. He had the content heart of a farmer and worked congenially beside Papa. Nick had soil in his blood and was gifted when it came to keeping the land productive.

Looking back, Will could understand the grief it must have caused his parents to see children peeling away from the homeplace out of their control and protection. He'd never lost the strong pull of Papa's hopes. It was no secret he prayed for them to all come home one day and claim their places.

Willheim well-remembered the day he'd ridden away

from the nest on the old plow horse. The plan had been for young Will to sell the sway-backed mare for whatever he could get and keep the money as a small stake.

So foolishly ashamed had he been of the old horse, he'd shortsightedly sold her to the first homesteader showing an interest once he was within walking distance of Sonora. He kept his tack and gear which became a laborious burden and a big mistake he'd never forget.

He entered the realm of cowboys on foot, weary, and loaded down because he wanted to save himself from the ridicule of riding an elderly horse. In hindsight, it only made him a bigger target for jokes.

A half-dead plug between his legs would have made little difference in his presentation. He could have saved himself from the painful, watery blisters bursting on his tender feet and the absolute exhaustion of toting his gear! Anything he had done or said caused humiliation for the first weeks of hazing anyway.

In the end, persevering and proving he was tenacious, trustworthy, and a person of good character who was slow to anger were the only things he had to prove.

Eddy Flores, the trail boss, rounded up his hands for an inspection. He wanted to see their guns first, of which Will didn't have even one. Next, he looked over their clothing, tack, and other gear. Will's pitiful possessions were most lacking.

There were fifteen men not counting the cook, biscuit roller, the outfit's wrangler, and the boss. Red Dandridge was the El Segundo. Loosely translated in Spanish the term meant the second man in charge or the ramrod.

Willheim soon learned several of the hands had ridden with Flores several times before and were tried and proven to be expert hands. Flores must have been a good boss, or none of them would have signed on with him repeatedly.

Eddy Flores hadn't paid attention or even spoken to Willheim until he ordered, "Come see me!"

The boy nodded and followed the man posthaste. Will was well aware he did not have the things he needed. He braced himself to be let go before he even got started. However, Flores handed him his first month's pay in advance. It amounted to $25.00. This was more cash money than he'd ever held in his hands before!

What would Papa think of such easy money?

"Don't worry, you'll urn ever cent of it, Kid. Put it way down deep 'n yer pocket with this here list a things I s'pect ya ta have before ya bed down tanight."

The boy was speechless. Before he could get his mouth to work and say his thanks, the boss pulled out a gun and gun belt for him to borrow.

"Put this outta sight 'til I get one'a tha men to teach ya how ta use it. He'll tell ya about possible situations ya might hav need uv it. This'll be a mighty rough trip. Ya kin't ride unarmed."

Neither Willheim or Flores could have foreseen the boy would save the boss's life someday with this very gun.

CHAPTER 3

BOSS OF THE PLAINS

The wrangler helped Willheim cut a horse out of the remuda. Will was anxious to get to the general store with a young cowboy named Adam Tanner. The money was burning a hole in his pocket, and he couldn't wait to buy what would be his most valuable possessions on this earth.

Adam Tanner was only a few weeks older than Will, but he was already a bona fide cowboy because this wasn't his first drive. He'd started working as the cook's molly with Flores when he was fourteen and orphaned. Will and Adam became instant friends and bunking buddies because of their closeness in age.

Adam had a speech impediment. He stuttered. He'd start out saying something rhythmically fine, but then words would stall and pile up on the tip of his tongue until he fairly spit them all out at once in a rush. He was far from being simple headed. He was smart.

It hadn't gone unnoticed by Will how the men never made fun of Adam's labored speech. On the contrary, they patiently listened and waited until his words spilled forth.

He was never excluded from a conversation, but rather, an effort was made to include him. Their deliberate regard for Adam got Will's attention. It was when he realized the older cowboys were actually kind and wise men. Their patience influenced all of the younger men by example.

After he recognized the pecking order of this new society, he was now a part, it made him more determined to be accepting of the ribbing and jokes tossed his direction and to laugh with the men. Initiating an inexperienced newbie was a normal, good-natured ritual.

The fellows clearly drew a line between razzing someone who didn't have a disability and someone who had an impairment and needed encouragement. Will started hearing the jokes at his expense for what they were. He quit taking offense and being resentful. This was another one of those important lessons he learned.

The only general store in the small town was stocked to outfit cowboys, farmers, pioneers, and homemakers. The long, narrow room got darker the farther back the merchandise was stacked. Every possible space was overflowing with practical goods, but at the same time it was tidy and organized. The balding storekeeper nodded in solemn acknowledgement and continued his work behind a counter arranging shelves of canned goods.

The bright blue and red bandanas in silk paisley prints or plain cotton cloth caught Will's eye first. Of all the items a cowboy might own, wear, or keep close at hand, nothing served more practical and versatile purposes than the twenty-inch squares commonly called wild rags. They were a standard part of a cowboy's attire and were used for work as well as social occasions. The squares were folded once to form a triangle and tied in front of the neck or in back of the neck in a square knot.

The huge kerchiefs were tools of the trade and were used as temporary saddle rigging, to cover the eyes of a spooked horse, or for washing and doctoring. Cowhands wore them foremost to cover their mouths and noses in all kinds of extreme weather or to avoid eating dust when riding drag and as head covers.

Bandanas were good rags for wiping off dirt, sweat, or blood. They were used as tourniquets, arm slings, and bandages. The handy squares made strong tie downs for anything needing to be secured. Cowboys used them to strain drinking water, as potholders, or for bundling food. They were even spread as makeshift tablecloths and sufficed as napkins.

Will started his pile on the scarred counter with two cotton bandanas. One was red and the other blue. He proceeded down the list of items Flores instructed him to buy. Adam Tanner left him alone for the most part but would sometimes nod his approval or shake his head in disagreement with his friend as the pile grew.

He selected a heavy shirt made of soldier blue flannel with a row of black buttons coming up from the bottom, across the top, and back down the front providing an extra layer of cloth. It made the shirt front stronger, practical, and stylish. Two pair of sturdy jeans, two pair of long johns, and four pair of wool socks along with a pair of sturdy boots, and leather gauntlet gloves were selected next.

A good supply of socks was necessary because a cowboy had to protect his feet above all else. To do this, it was wise to keep feet as clean and dry as possible under harsh conditions. No foot, no horse, no foot, no cowboy was a wise thing to remember in the west!

Buying a two-dollar Stetson made Will feel like a real cowboy and much larger in stature than the scrawny boy he was. Cowboys dressed the same except for the way they shaped their hats. How they steamed, creased, and molded the pliable brims and crowns spoke of a man's attitude.

He knew little of the manufacturer's name, John B. Stetson, but Adam educated him. The company was founded in Philadelphia in 1865 by a young man who learned the trade of hat making from his father.

When he was a youth, the boy was sickly and suffered acute bouts of respiratory distress. Doctors back east agreed his best chances for healing his lungs lay to the west where the air was said to be dry as a bone. It was true! In time the arid climate dried his lungs out.

While regaining strength in the arid climate, he became fascinated by the individual ways cowboys pinched and molded the shapes of their hats. The overall effects spoke volumes about their attitudes and identities even from a distance.

John had helped his father make hats, and he was a thinker. He pondered the idea of a blank felt hat catering to western customers deciding their own preferences. A plain blank hat could be bent and molded in response to the wearers' varied likes and personalities.

When he returned back east, his idea of the basic hat took legs. He named it The Boss of the Plains! It hit the western market running and quickly became Stetson's fastest selling model. It came with a domed, nondescript crown, a pronounced straight brim, and no hint of factory styling. It provided cowboys with a blank canvas to style for themselves.

As Will stood before these basic Stetsons with Adam, he picked one of the earthier colors. He chose a buckskin color lighter than his reddish-brown hair. He selected a narrow, black leather band with one silver Concho from another rack.

Last on the list was a fish, which was a long rain jacket. Adam threw the yellow, rubbery rain slicker on the pile. Will asked why it was called a fish, and Adam pointed to the small fish embossed on the back, just under the collar.

The old, grizzled storekeeper tallied up the bill and wrapped the goods in brown paper bundles tied with string. His pretty Mexican wife looked as young as the boys. Will felt sorry for her because she had no smile and kept her eyes downcast.

The gruff-mannered man in a dirty shop apron treated her like a slave, and she complied without a sound. She never looked up at Will or Adam. Will didn't have a chance to offer her a look of understanding.

He had gained so much knowledge from the small bits and pieces of information he'd learned. Will made a mental note to always be Adam Tanner's friend.

At the livery stable, the two boys looked over the used saddles left by the deceased or drifters looking for a few dollars to spend. Sometimes farmers or drifters came upon hard times and needed cash to pay bills or move out of the territory.

Will tried three of them on the back of his horse until Adam was satisfied it fit and had a thousand miles of wear left in it. Will traded Papa's saddle and bridle plus a dollar for ones more fitting of a Texas cowboy.

Now, he was completely outfitted except for a lariat rope. Adam had two and offered his new acquaintance the use of one along with free lessons on how to use it.

Will had been able to outfit himself with a small sum of money left over. Only one of the extra dollars found its way into his pocket adding to the scant funds from the sale of his plow horse. He'd tuck them into the inside band of his new hat later for safer keeping. He truly felt like a rich and independent man.

Will slipped into an empty stall and changed into his new duds, but he saved the bright, blue shirt for a more fitting time, choosing to wear one of his Ma's homemade shirts. He carefully rolled up his new and old belongings in the brown paper from the store.

Before mounting the horse, he reached down and picked up a little dust to rub onto his new britches. Then he lightly scuffed the new leather of his sharp-toed boots. He looked up to see the already mounted Adam watching him.

They grinned at each other. Both knew he wanted to hide some of the newness of his gear. Maybe the men wouldn't rib him so much for the new duds.

The two friends rode toward a saloon at the end of the street. Above the entry was a crude, hand painted sign with green letters. It read, **"BUG JUICE."** One of the rickety swinging doors was only attached by the top hinge causing it to hang cockeyed. Regulars with rummy eyes stared at them but quickly lost interest. The room was small, dark, and needed sweeping.

Adam ordered two beers. He threw a nickel for each expertly on the counter in such a way it rolled before falling flat on the makeshift bar. Will was impressed with his skill and made a mental note to learn how to do this.

The warm, weak, dingy liquid with no froth was a far cry from the homemade German ale his parents were famous for making, but he drank it all the way down anyway. It was wet but tasted raunchy. For the first time since leaving home, Will was homesick.

In the scheme of things, an unknown future stretched many miles and years ahead of him.

Chapter 4

Sweetwater, Texas

Willheim's thoughts flashed forward to the present as the actual miles left to go today had grown shorter. This was not the end of the journey he'd taken to become a man for he was sure he had much more to learn.

He felt like he'd completed a full circle at least and was right back where he'd started but at a new beginning. He must figure out how to approach this whole new chapter in the story of his life.

He was riding Rope Tail, the strongest horse he'd ever worked. This black, muscled mustang gelding was sold to him by Wild Ned Mason. The horse and Ned's three brush dogs had always been together. The four animals had bonded and were a set.

The bossy old authoritarian thought he was in control of the four animals and was dumbfounded when his dogs refused to leave Rope Tail behind. After ordering, hollering, and even sweet-talking, they never offered to budge an inch from the horse he'd sold to Brandt.

Disgusted, Wild Ned had put his hands up in the air

and spat on the ground as he cursed loudly. "Damn, useless animuls anyway, goldarned happy ta be shed of 'em. The lousy mongrels er yers ta feed, Will, they's yer problem now."

He rode off in a cloud of dust like the fire of hell had been lit under him! Willheim had only crossed paths with the grumpy wrangler once after the dog fiasco. It had been almost three years since he'd last seen or even heard of him. He assumed the most infamous horse wrangler in all of West Texas, Wild Ned Mason, had kicked the bucket.

Willheim and his small caravan sloshed across the Red River into familiar territory yesterday. Riding through the familiar mesquite trees cleared Will's head and brought invigorated clarity to his plans.

His heart quickened with only a few more miles to go before reaching Sweetwater. This journey was as good as over. The barren, winter terrain might look like nought to a newcomer, but to Will it was the place he loved. No ground was as grand, and no people were as dear to his heart.

Rustling from the undergrowth broke the silence. Red Dog, Indigo, and Blacksmith burst through the thicket making racket and disturbing the birds. The dogs greeted their horse and master with high-pitched squeals and raucous noises of reunion.

"Well, ole' boys, where ya'll been up to? Must a been rustling up your own grub as y'all've been scarce as hen's teeth taday. I bet ya'll can tell we er might near ta home.

"As soon as ya have tha hankering, take off 'n' beat me ta Meta Anna's kitchen door. I 'spect she's waitin' fer y'all right now with juicy scraps ah plenty. The young'uns 'ill turn ya'll into reg'lar old sorry house pets once they git hands on ya!" he drawled to the yippy dogs.

As if understanding what he'd said, they settled and waited for biscuits, wagging their tails. He tossed out the last three he'd saved back for them. After gobbling the offerings, they took off on a run.

No doubt he wouldn't see Indigo, Red Dog, and Blacksmith again until he made it home. No doubt the pack was on its way to Papa's yard. When his dogs showed up, anyone at home would know Will made it to Sweetwater.

His brush dogs were peculiar critters. They were the meanest, toughest pack of brush dogs Will had ever seen. On a trail drive the three together could root out the worst maverick steers from the thickest, thorniest draws and get them neatly pointed in the right direction.

On the tall grass prairie, the hounds mostly foraged off the land eating small varmints. When they reached Meta's kitchen stoop, it was a different story. Those dogs transformed into a gentle, pesky band of beggars. At Meta Anna's backdoor, they watched for handouts like the Rat Row derelicts in town.

They'd lean into the nieces and nephews and let them do anything to them. The kids could pick bugs and cockleburs out of their coats. They could wash and comb their tangled fur, tie goofy bows around their necks, and lead them around by strings of yarn.

Children and dogs shared a language only they understood. Together, they made joyous sounds running around carefree, playing games, and acting silly. He never begrudged these quirky work dogs the few chances they had to just be treated like farm pets.

After leaving his horses at the livery, it was always Will's routine to stop at Ely's general store for fresh duds before heading over to the bath house. Next, he'd get his hair under control at the barber shop. Then, he'd heading over to see Lizzy, at the fanciest whorehouse this side of Fort Worth, The House of Satin.

This time, he wouldn't be seeking pleasure at the tricked-up house where Elizabeth was employed. It would only be for a blunt, to the point talk with Elizabeth Hartley. What he had to say was weighing heavily on his mind. He wasn't going for playtime with the beautiful, petite

Elizabeth Hartley. He hoped she'd take the news in stride.

Will shook his head bitterly as the pathetic rhyme he had made up long ago repeated itself in his head.

Sweet, little Eliza,
the sweetheart of many,
passed from one sap to plenty
all for the price of a penny!

Most cowboys weren't particular where they found a woman to bed. They had no qualms about taking advantage of them and bragged about their deceitfulness around the campfires. Without remorse, they soiled lonely widows, abused saloon doves, and paid for brothel services.

Will had dreamed of experiencing these escapades with someone close to his age. On his first winter trip home, he heard talk of a beautiful girl at The House of Satin. With money in his pocket, he had started visiting her secretly even though his Christian conscience plagued him night and day.

To appease his guilt, he misled her with hints he might marry her when he retired from pushing cattle. Somehow, the bait made him feel justified. Now his sensibility wouldn't allow him to keep up the charade.

Lizzy was more overjoyed with the little white lies Willheim had told her than he had thought she would be. The marriage idea snowballed over the years until Lizzy made plans. He had no idea if he'd ever want to leave the trail behind, so marrying her was no threat to him. In fact, it made it easier to play along with the deception and enjoy her attentions to the fullest. Last year, he'd realized too late the mistake he'd made stringing her along so convincingly.

Satin was a high-class, professional operation and the finest, cleanest, most discreet of such businesses. Eliza was gorgeous and had expertly developed her trade with him as well as others. Her stunning looks, expertise, and ravenous passions kept him from pouring cold water on the idea he would someday marry her.

What a mess he'd created with his silence. Now, he'd have to tell her the truth of his deception once and for all. He hated the thought of cutting their ties, but she wasn't the sort of woman he could marry, nor did he want her to give birth to his children.

Willheim Brandt was set on finding a decent woman to marry and start a family. The idea had been taking up more and more acreage in his head ever since Adam Tanner's sorrowful death. What happened to him could happen to Will. Being a cowboy was a hard, dangerous way to make a living.

He'd pondered if he had an obligation to marry Lizzy, but he decided against it. She was the one who had chosen to make a living on her back. She'd lain under one man after another all this time and participated in unspeakable acts contrary to his upbringing. She was a whole lot of fun but nothing else to him.

Plain and simple, any cowpoke who laid money on Madam Nadine's counter as he came in the door could have her. He liked Elizabeth, but he could never marry a prostitute or take her home to his family. Hell's bells, his mother would turn over in her grave!

At night on a trail drive lonely cowboys bragged about the women waiting for them at the end of the line. Whether real or fabricated, no one cared, as long as the stories were interesting. Lizzy was the fodder of his tales. The men enjoyed fantasizing about beautiful ladies, theirs or someone else's. It was one of the ways they coped with the loneliness of the prairie.

Only once, when he was stranded in a blizzard, did Will talk himself into being in love with her. After he didn't freeze to death, he started thinking straight quickly. He deplored the way she made her money. What if he lied to her about his affections? He had paid up for every favor.

Reining Rope Tail to a halt brought the three other horses tethered behind to gently pile up against each other. No scene soothed Will's eyes more readily than the vista spread before him. The main thoroughfare of Sweetwater sliced through town all the way to the Texas & Pacific Depot. He could see people scurrying about their business on horses, wagons, and on foot.

The next street over was Rat Row where the idle homeless loitered during the day and milled around like rats at night. It was where Sweetwater's five rowdy saloons, dance halls, pool parlors, and common ladies of the evening hung out.

Will's animals bobbed their heads and backed up a step or two with front hooves pawing the ground nervously. They shied a bit at the distant noises and unsavory smells civilization produced. Their nostrils contracted and expelled short, breathy puffs of air. With heads tilted up, they rumbled soft whickers.

He agreed the unavoidable stenches of smoke hanging above the town and odors from the ditches dug to drain raw sewage away were nasty byproducts of a society living closely together. The smells didn't deter Will from waving his hat above his head and letting out a loud whoop and holler as he spurred Rope Tail forward pushing him and the others into fast clips.

As he entered town, many citizens milled around, and he raised his hand or nodded a few greetings with big grins. No matter how anxious he was to stop and chew the fat with a few, he resisted the temptation. Will would have plenty of time for talking later. He made a beeline to the livery stable to drop off his stock.

"Hellooo, Meekin!" he hollered. "Get your sorry, no count, onery hide out here and help a cowboy with money in his jeans!"

He dismounted, giving release to another loud whoop. Soon everyone in Sweetwater would know he'd hit town.

Meekin, the owner, appeared in the sunshine against the backdrop of a double-wide, darkened doorway. The big barn-like structure sat handily beside the blacksmith's shop where it was most needed.

"Well, tarnation, if it ain't young Will his self! Your pa'll be glad as punch ya made it back in one piece in time fer Christmas. He sure needs ya home."

Meekin was a good-hearted old soul, a jolly man by nature. Will had known him his whole life. He noticed the man wasn't as jubilantly talkative as usual, and the grin on his face didn't quite reach his eyes. When he next opened his mouth again to speak, shaking his head slightly, he closed his it only waving a hand in greeting.

Will was so happy to be home, he overlooked his friend's awkward behavior.

"Put my critters up and store their loads. Tell your hired hand ta curry 'em, clean their feet, and grain 'em good. Oh, and toss 'em hay.

I'll be back to visit with ya later. I got ta get the dust and grime cleaned off! You wouldn't like bein' too close to me just now!" Will laughed.

"I bet yer right 'bout that. Get on outta here 'n' rent a tub, ya look more like a grizzly than a no-good cowboy," he laughed half-heartedly as he led the horses into the dark mouth of the livery.

Chapter 5

Bad News!

After a dunk and frothy scrub in a tin tub at the communal bathhouse, he was feeling like a new man. The steaming hot water and a white cake of homemade soap had done wonders. Will felt clean and smelled one hundred percent better! He dried with the toweling handed to him by the matron and donned brand-new clothing from the skin out. He finished off with a new pair of boots. He felt rejuvenated!

His spirits momentarily took a dive when he glimpsed his reflection in the barbershop mirror. It had been over two months since he'd seen himself. His long hair and thick beard were both way past due for the shears. Longhorns on the prairie or a cowpoke's horse didn't care how a man looked, only how he treated his animals.

The freshly washed, rich-colored, reddish-brown hair reached past his shoulders in wild, unkept locks. A matted mass of stiff whiskers grew every which way covering his face. He looked more like a trapper from the hills than a man in the market for decent wife.

He contritely sat down in the barber's chair causing it to squeak under his weight. Mr. Roderman, the barber, tsked, tsked and commenced talking incessantly and laughing at his own jokes, all the while expertly weeding.

He started with an oversized pair of scissors and whacked off hair letting it fall to the floor. Then, he changed to a smaller pair, snipping closer and shaping. When he finished, it lay nicely ruffled on the top.

He trimmed the rest of it until it waterfalled at his jawline. Roderman continued combing and making adjustments until at last he called it finished. This whole time he'd been rattling gossip mixed with bits news and bigger bits of town gossip.

Shaving the disarrayed beard took another set of skills. After chopping the bulk of the wiry facial hair, he lathered Willheim up until he looked like a dead ringer for a snowman. This whole time the barber had kept a steady stream of opinions flowing.

Mr. Roderman turned to sharpen a straight razor on the leather strop hanging on the wall.

Will interrupted him. "Roderman, leave me a big mustache. I'm partial to havin' one."

The barber laughed and said, "You're in luck, Son, this I can do. Mustachios are my specialty!"

Will was only half listening, and barely following along until Roderman dropped an anvil!

"I sure was sorry to hear about Tavias. The whole town is grieving right along with your family. I've never heard a bad word spoken about any of you Brandt boys. He will be missed."

It was fortunate the shave was finished because Will pulled off the dingy sheet using it to wipe the remnants of white lather away. He jumped to his feet hard enough to make the wooden floor vibrate. He wadded up the cloth and tossed it away.

"Repeat what ya just said ta me, Roderman. Surely, I

misheard ya!

"Go on and tell me the straight of it. What happened to Tavy?"

"Oh, when will I ever learn to keep my flappin' mouth shut? Will, I thought for sure ya already knew! I am so sorry you have to hear it from me."

"Yer brother, Tavy, is dead. I don't know the whole story, but it happened at Adobe Wall in the Pan Handle. Sit back down and let me finish, then you can be on your way."

"You are finished!"

Will slammed some coins down on the counter.

"This should cover the haircut and shave."

"Go talk ta yer family, Will. It's too bad 'a news ta hear sittin' in a barber's chair. I don't know the whole story. Truly, l don't!" Roderman said.

Will had already turned his back to the man and forgotten him as he exited onto the street and slammed the door behind him.

He didn't know what to believe, not until he knew for sure. His mind refused to process any of this. It couldn't possibly be true. He made long, fast tracks to the general store for Savannah Grace to verify or deny it.

When he went to see Savannah at the store earlier, Ely was clearly swamped. He was minding the store by himself and trying to deal with several customers at once. He managed to quickly tell him Savanah was out with the children and to take what he wanted. They could settle up later.

Right now, Will was shaky and had the body of a rag after the water had been wrung out of it. Considering the possibility he might vomit; he realized his stomach was reminding him it was empty. All of a sudden, he was starving and badly in need of food.

Will decided fill his belly first and go see his sister after he calmed down. Until then, he'd allow himself to keep thinkng Roderman was mistaken. He talked so much he'd probably got his stories mixed up.

Surely, Ely would have taken the time to tell him this news if it was the actual truth.

Willheim didn't want to chance running into anyone he knew. He wasn't in a talking mood and wouldn't be until he got the straight of what he'd heard. Will ducked into an ally to avoid running into someone he knew. He'd go someplace out of the way.

Hands down, Pedro Juantez served the best fried chicken in three counties. His small café was on a back, short street, no more than a lane, really. Will had eaten his fill of beans and bacon for too long. He made his way down the alley to a little, rutted side street until the heavy aroma of comfort food hit him. The smells of fry bread, fried potatoes, and fried chicken reeled him in.

He pushed the sagging door. It scrapped over an unevenly packed dirt floor as it opened. The familiar jingling of the little Mexican brass bells was inviting. They had hung at the top of it for as long as Will could remember. The sound triggered happy thoughts of his brothers and him coming here over the years.

The primitive cafe was frozen in time and hadn't changed one iota from the past. The same greasy, yellow calico curtains still hung limply over two streaked and greasy front windows. In the corner, covered with a thick cloth, was Pedro's tall, thirty-six string harp. People for miles around hired him to play at funerals, weddings, dances, tea parties, and revivals.

Not only was the smell of fried foods intense, but he could hear hot grease sizzling behind the thick curtain separating the customers from the kitchen. Everything cooked here by Pedro's children was fried. He sat down at an empty side table shoved against the adobe wall leaving his Stetson on his head.

Pedro sauntered over to the table wearing his own

grease-stained cowboy hat and a grimy cook's apron. Grinning lazily, he offered a greeting.

"Ah, buenos dias mi amigo, Brandt. Que paso, tu' a la deriva gringo."

"Feliz Navidad, yourself, ole amigo! Fry a hungry man some chicken and play a Christmas tune or two on yer geetar while your boys cook," Will smiled at the man, but his mind was on Tavy, and his mood was dour.

Pedro could sure pick a guitar. He played two songs fit for the ears of God's angels. Will leaned back with his legs stretched out long in front of him and his big arms crossed. With his eyes closed, he let the mellow music drift over him. For a moment he was at peace.

Pedro's son, Danny, walked out from behind the curtain with the fried carne de el pollo, and Will's stomach growled when he set up. The full plate was enough to give him a pause. It was loaded with the best parts of chicken, crispy and golden, fried potatoes, and pillows of hot fry bread with honey.

Will cleaned the plate and washed it down with hot, black coffee strong enough to grow hair on his chest. He pushed away from the table, throwing money down for his food and the entertainment. Anyone within earshot heard him say, "Gracias, Adios!"

Savannah Grace should be back in the store by now, so he headed there. Indeed, she was behind the counter in the throes of a somber discussion with a pushy salesman over questionable business. Willheim had entered unnoticed and watched his sister hold her ground. He couldn't keep from grinning as he observed his sister-cousin handling the slick drummer.

Savannah had quite a head for business, and the black-suited dry goods hawker quit trying to outtalk her. He finally closed the catalogue and snapped his salesman's case shut. He walked out shaking his head and mumbling a disgruntled comment under his breath.

Savannah looked up and saw her brother waiting. She lifted up the partition in the counter and ran straight into his open arms.

"Ooh, Will, Will! Ely said you'd made it home. I just couldn't believe it! Let me look at you. Mmm, you smell good, for a cowboy! My husband must have lied about you being dirty," she laughed.

"Nah, it was no lie. Savannah Grace, you're a sight for sore eyes. I just can't get enough of looking at you. Goodness, Girl are you in the family way again? You and Ely are going to have a full house before I ever even get my family started!"

She admonished, "Well, a fellow has to stay at home long enough to find a girl and get married. A man as handsome of face and as smooth talking as you, would have no trouble finding the right gal if he tried."

"Lately, I've been thinking on tha same thing, tryin', I mean. Funny, you should bring it up!

"Savannah, what's this I just heard at tha barbershop 'bout Tavy? It ain't true, is it?"

She dropped her eyes, and a small, delicate hand came up to cover her mouth. Tears filled the wells of her eyes before she laid her head on his chest.

"Come with me, Will" she whispered. "I'll send Sam out to watch the front for a while, I reckon he can handle it. We need to talk in private."

The two entered the Benton family's living quarters hidden behind the thick, gray, sackcloth curtain. It was a comfortable apartment, tidy, and well furnished. Marrying Ely Benton had been a very good thing for his gentle sister.

The children swamped their uncle immediately with hugs and kisses, and they squealed when he pretended to fall on the floor. The sight of the kids brought him great pleasure. Being a proud uncle, Will carried on over each child's growth and handsome face.

When they quieted down, Savannah sent Sam, her

oldest child, up front to help his pa. She shooed Ella off with the smaller two.

"Take your sisters to the kitchen table, Darlin', and read stories to them, so Uncle Willheim and I can talk. Let them have milk and sugar cookies, please."

"I'm sorry, Will, but you know how tender Ely's heart is. He can't even wring a mean rooster's neck. He should have told you when you got here.

"Yes, Brother, word has reached us of Tavy's death. I don't know how much you know, so I'll start from the beginning. Whatever you were told, there's likely to be some truth in it. What exactly did you hear?"

"Not much, Roderman told me he was sorry ta hear 'bout Tavy, an' he was worried 'bout how Papa was takin' it. I was so shocked, and I don't remember what else he said. Once he realized I didn't know what happened, his lips shut up tighter than a jug lid on tha subject. He wouldn't discuss Tavy further.

"Afterwards, I stayed clear a anyone who might bring Tavy's name up. I wanted ta talk ta you first. I'm guessin' somethin' terrible's gone wrong. "It's bad, ain't it?"

"Why, this has might near killed our papa! It aged him overnight." Savannah covered her entire face with her hands and wept bitterly into them. Between sobs, words gushed out in spurts. "Tavy stole---a horse---up in the panhandle! He took the horse---then hung himself---at the Adobe Wall jail---after---after---he'd been locked up---for being a horse---thief!

"He committed---suicide, Will! He must have---must have---been so ashamed---of what---what---he'd done. The law was---going to hang him---anyway!"

Will wiped the tears off of Savannah's face with his bandana and then just stared up at the ceiling for over a minute, at least.

"Naw, there ain't no way anything you said could a happened. Tavy's not a thief. He wouldn't take another man's horse. He's not a coward neither. Tavy wouldn't kill his self. He'd never do it. There's no way what ya'll heard could a happened! No way!"

"I don't want to believe it either, but the word Papa got was from the sheriff. He'd gotten a telegram from the law at Adobe Wall."

"Papa is waiting for everyone to get home, and then he wants you boys to go and fetch Tavy's body home after Christmas---bring him to rest beside Mama." She choked on more sobs.

"I can't talk anymore, Will. Don't ask me to speculate. You go on now and take care of your business in town before you go out to the homeplace.

"Meta Anna won't be looking for you before tonight or tomorrow. I reckon those dogs of yours are already out there lying around like company and begging for handouts.

"Papa definitely knows you'll be there soon too." She smiled at him through weepy eyes.

"Take some time for this to sink in before Papa sees you. He'll need your strength. I believe all the others are already with him, even Kat! Pa has plenty of support at the moment.

"The dogs always signal you're close, so he's been alerted. Those mangy hounds are worth their weight in gold to this family! They mean Christmas time to all the children.

"My bunch will be out on Christmas Eve. We'll have to have the store open Christmas Eve morning, but we'll close at noon. We make a lot of sales then.

"This is a sad time for everyone, but all the kids need the usual holidays even with Tavy gone. They're too young to understand the gravity of what's happened and don't know the details. Besides, a tragedy and loss like this reminds a us how precious our time is with each other."

"Yeah, well, Savannah, I've been thinking on how fast tha time ticks away from us even before I heard of this sorrow. It's time I stuck around Sweetwater to build a house on my own spread. I want a wife, young'uns, and a future."

After Will confided his plans, he departed with slightly stooped shoulders.

Savannah made tracks behind him to the door and stared after her brother until he disappeared into the bank. Shaking her head at what he'd just shared, she went back and relieved Sam at the counter.

Will confiding in her about marrying was surprising. It was a happy thing to think about amid all this heartache.

Chapter 6

A Voice from the Grave

Will meant to transfer the sum of his earnings into his bank account in Sweetwater, but as he passed through the heavy door, sudden grief reared its ugly head and ripped through him. The death of his closest brother, his best friend in the world, picked this inopportune moment to threaten to spill out of his heart. The last thing he needed was to break down in the bank with an audience.

To keep his breakdown private, he walked straight past the tellers without looking to the right or to the left. The back door leading to the alleyway offered the opportunity to find the solitude a crying man needed.

He barely cleared and shut the door before his grief flooded over in a giant gush, and he could hardly get his breath. This had never happened to him before. He put his back against the rough, uneven, cold stones of the bank wall and slid downward until he was sitting on the ground.

His head was down on a bent knee, and a fist was jammed against his mouth to muffle the pitiful sounds of agony. Will sat alone in the sun freely crying tears of loss and regret for Tavy from his breached heart.

After the tide of his pain was spent, he took his bandana, still damp from Savannah's tears, to wipe away his own tears for Tavias. Relief had come from the dam bursting, and he was able to regain his composure.

He walked to the livery stable to collect his friend, Rope Tail. The money transfer could wait. He rode the black mustang away at a fast clip and galloped on the open prairie outside of town. When Will ran low on steam, he circled around and tied his horse in front of the bank.

He passed once again through the bank door as if nothing had happened and took care of the deposit. If possible, Will didn't intend to cry for Tavy again, but he was damn determined to find the real truth behind Tavy's death and clear his brother's name.

Later in the Blue Goose Post Office, Will checked for mail in General Delivery under his name. A clerk he didn't recognize handed him a small bundle of scripts and papers through the window of a shiny metal cage. He walked over to where the light was better and shuffled through the stack.

A familiar letter from Eddy Flores caused the corners of his mouth to lift with fondness. Flores was his first trail boss. He had taken the time to teach this skinny boy all things important about cowboying and many things about being a man.

Without thinking, Willheim dropped a gentle hand to the Colt single action Army revolver hanging low on his hip. Flores had loaned him this piece before he even knew how to load it, much less use it. The revolver represented a monumental moment in the past when the difference between life and death was only a matter of seconds.

When the time came to return the gun, Flores refused to take it back. This gun represented the lasting bond they had formed. Like real friends do, they still kept track of each other.

The next envelope was from a name Will recognized as

another trail boss he didn't know as well. No doubt this man wanted a commitment from him to ride for his outfit in the spring. He'd write a note back to thank him for the offer but declare his time on the trail was done.

There were a few adverts and such he saved to peruse later. The rest of this mail could wait as well for a better time to sort through it, except for a singular envelope, soiled, crumpled, dirty, and bulkier than the others. Thin, lightweight writing paper was used for most posts. Out of all the mail, this particular envelope captured his curiosity. He struggled to juggle it to the top of the pile he was holding in one hand but was frustrated when it and other pieces of mail slipped to the floor landing at his feet.

He bent and gathered it all up again with the one he wanted on top of the pile. Aside from the soiled, messy condition setting it apart, it also didn't have the sender's name, or a return address noted on the outside of the envelope. The postmark was from Albuquerque, Texas and dated several weeks back. This was not a standard letter.

What the hell?

Albuquerque was in Gonzales County, just east of San Antonio. Will's name and Sweetwater, Texas were written in expansive, penciled print sprawled across the front of the grimy envelope. His curiosity took over, and he ripped open the tenuous seal. He didn't expect the contents to be what looked like a partial piece of cracked and worn boot lining!

Scratched crudely into the brittle, stained pasteboard were words rubbed with soot to make the message more visible.

Well, this just beats all! I'll be damned if Tavy didn't send this!

When he first deciphered the scratches, the words were delivered to his mind in Tavy's own voice.

Tavy, I swear I can hear you, my brother!

Tavy's mentally audible words chilled Willheim to the

bone. They made absolutely no sense to him, but he knew Tavias was trying to speak to him from the grave! Puzzled by the mystery, he stuffed it deep into his shirt pocket to keep it safe

He had a loose end he had ignored far too long. The situation with Elizabeth Hartley absolutely had to be tied up this afternoon. As soon as this mistake was erased, he'd focus entirely on what Tavias wanted him to know!

Chapter 7

The House of Satin

~Nadine Welch

The House of Satin sat like a beacon on a rolling prairie hill, and it looked to the outside world like the property of a banker, wealthier than sin. As with many things the devil has used for bait over the ages, it was an illusion promising grandiose treasures held within its shiny walls.

It appeared as an oasis nestled in the tall grass prairie. Its elegance pulled in rich, famous, and influential men from near and far away. Even a cowboy like Willheim Brandt with money in the bank, land of his own, and a prominent last name to boot could enter. Discretion and secrecy were always guaranteed.

This was a house of iniquity, and the owner was more cunning than any man. A variety of illicit thrills was on the menu to entice men with deep pockets to turn loose of their cash. It was owned and operated by a wicked woman on the take.

It belonged solely to Madam Nadine Welch and full of

everything fine. She kept it stocked with addictive sweets of honey, nectar, and liquor. She filled it with beautiful women offered up to satisfy the devil's own appetite.

Nadine Welch had elevated herself from the ashes until she had become the wealthiest businesswoman in West Texas. It was uncommon for a woman to reach such financial heights in a man's world, especially since she'd pulled herself up from so little.

Nadine started as a mistreated, unnamed waif in a county orphanage. She had suffered there under horrible taskmasters. She escaped only to end up an even poorer whore lying on her back in dark alleys for meager compensation. She was nothing but a pitiful, homeless whore, until one day a sweet-talking businessman of sorts invited her to eat, live, and work in his big house. The big house turned out to be a bawdy bordello, and it wasn't much of a promotion from the streets, but still, it was better.

So be it. She was shrewd like a rat and used this as an opportunity, a steppingstone. She went about her business without complaining, but all the while she was learning about the operational business end of things. Nadine made the sweet-talking man in the alley more money than any other girl he'd ever graduated into his house.

She quietly gleaned knowledge about the inner workings of high society and the power of money for those few who had it. It didn't take long to figure out working for the house was a dead end. She wanted more money and more power. The real golden calf was in owning her own place with a special and unique flavor wealthy and famous men would sell their souls to experience.

She became the genius and essence behind the doors of The House of Satin. It was her own creation with a magical array of beauties and sin to suit every taste and fulfill every fantasy. She prospered, and her reputation grew right along with The House of Satin. Customers frequented her place from as far away as Ft. Worth, Dallas, and farther.

These days, the enormous three-story building always looked as if it had been freshly painted in three tones of mellow blues with crisp shudders, shining windows, a wraparound porch, and a groomed yard accented by white picket fences looking like piped frosting on a cake. Tidy outbuildings were staffed and provided shelter for keeping customers horses and conveyances out of sight and private.

Inside the house Victorian furniture, lacy curtains, and the clean aroma of lemon polish set mellowed in subdued lighting. This presentation showcased an atmosphere of elegance. The impressive, walnut counter in the main entrance hall was used to receive and direct guests and collect fees for services. It also served as a bar for drinks and smoking.

Beyond this entrance was a grand walnut, ornately carved spiral staircase. It loomed in all its glory like a great behemoth leading the way up to the bedrooms. They were staged with appropriate props, clean and beautiful beddings, extra pillows, classical books, and other accents to match specific themes.

Nadine's girls were educated and tutored in current events, demure etiquette, hygiene, makeup and hair styling. She indulged her girls in fine Southern style.

She truly trusted no other person but herself and managed the business, money, and screened incoming traffic at the door. The house catered to a much higher clientele than the general public. Nadine sought for the most affluent.

Madam Nadine's business sense and experience taught her a varied selection of products provided equal and better profits. She employed a bountifully mixed lot of fabulous girls to satisfy all men's vices, tastes, appetites, and to please unspoken fantasies. The glorious ladies had different proportions, hair colors, and personalities as well. Whatever filled her pocketbook to the brim was always her guide.

Most of her girls were white skinned but from different countries, both literally and feigned. A few were Mexican senoritas, and one, named Mavis, was an exquisite and exotic black girl. Mavis looked as if she'd just stepped out of the wiles of Africa. She joined the group only a month ago. She was a big-boned, ebony beauty. Nadine quickly gave her the title of The African Queen.

Nadine's intuition told her the girl was running from something. She recognized the panic and wariness in her eyes, but it made no difference to her. This was a good place to hide and get lost. The madam felt fortunate to have someone of such uncommonly striking stature.

The House of Satin also required practical staff to do domestic work, cooking, washing, and outside chores. She vetted anyone she employed. The menial staff, few in number, were selected quite carefully.

Nadine hired older, unmarried individuals with few outside contacts. There was little turnover because the pay and keep were both most generous in exchange for good work, total loyalty, and absolute secrecy. Anyone who had a job under the umbrella of The House of Satin protected it.

Nadine never considered her line of work to be wrong. Men sought frolics with females regardless, and maybe what she offered would keep some young, church girl from unwanted handling by a friend of the family. With this reasoning, what she offered for a price could actually be defined as public service.

A few of her girls eventually moved on to marry customers who visited them. Unattached ladies of refinement were scarce in the wilds of the rugged West Texas Plains, and The Satin certainly offered a living catalog of possibilities. Where else could a lonely gentlemen in the wilderness with few women find such a large smorgasbord of delicacies to taste and sample?

Now, Elizabeth Hartley was different. She was Nadine's pet, her favorite girl of all time. In fact, she loved her very own daughter. She had found the child working in a boarding house in Dallas at the age of twelve. She was abandoned and had no one to care for her. Her parents disappeared without telling her they were leaving. They vanished for parts unknown, and their child was ill equipped to fend for herself.

She was a beautiful angel-faced child forced to change soiled sheets, dust rooms, and empty slop jars day in and day out. Nadine fell in love with her porcelain, untouched, doll-like qualities at once. She befriended the girl and saved her from a penniless life of hard work, abuse, and misery.

Lizzy was near fourteen when, after much begging, Nadine agreed to let her work on The House of Satin floor. So young and angelic, the madam was hesitant at first, but immediately Lizzy noticed, and fistfuls of revenue started flowing into the till on her account. The girl loved the work so much she had to be forced to take a night off.

Once she hit twenty, Nadine knew even the brightest flames began to burn lower for a whore. Seven years of constantly servicing men was hard on a female, and it was time Elizabeth started making plans for the future.

It didn't go unnoticed by Nadine, when the girl turned her soulful eyes in the direction of the handsome young cowboy named Willheim Brandt. Nadine considered him to be a suitable match because of his well thought of family name. She had learned he was in line to inherit a sizable piece of rich land, and he was already employed.

If he'd only light in one place long enough to take root, an actual romance might bloom between Elizabeth and Will. He seemed to return the same favor of admiration young Lizzy carried on her sleeve for him.

Nadine would gladly give her blessings to the pair and provide a generous dowry to boot if he rescues her pet from a life of prostitution!

What better ending could there be for Elizabeth Hartley's story? It would be perfect!

CHAPTER 8

PRETTIEST GIRL ON THE FLOOR

~Willheim Brandt

Is the message something or is it nothing? What am I missing, Tavias? Surely, the scant words you wrote must mean something.

The bizarre, ragged piece of cardboard in Willheim's shirt pocket worried his thoughts. Was Tavy reaching out for something, maybe? The distorted letters made the words hard to read, and then they made no sense to Willheim.

Brother, what is it you're needing from me?

What meaning could the scant words possibly hold? Unanswered questions bombarded Will. He had lots of them but no answers. Pushing the mystery to the back of his mind was the only thing he could do right now.

Eliminating anything connecting his life to Elizabeth Hartley's life was a priority for the next few hours. He was guilty of stringing her along with talk of a future together. He'd been lying to her for years when there had never been the slightest chance he'd marry her. He had known it wasn't in the cards, and he figured Lizzy knew it too. At least, he hoped she had known the reality of their entanglement.

In his limited experience, he had no other prostitute with whom to compare Elizabeth Hartley. She was damn good at her profession, beautiful, and always willing to tumble. Lizzy was a whole lot of naughty fun.

Even though he paid for it every time, his conscience was bothering him. He really owed the girl no explanation for why he was quitting her, but he just wished he hadn't played the part of a suitor. For this reason, he planned to eat crow and apologize for any misunderstandings or hard feelings. Then he could forget about this chapter of his life.

Today, riding toward the grassy knoll, the blue backdrop of Sweetwater's Double Mountains didn't make the house stand out to greet him as they usually did. For the first time, he realized they never had.

Why have I been in awe of this house? I never saw the empty shell built on lies.

He deserved the confrontation ahead with his longtime mistress. He wasn't looking forward to it. His part in this charade was a grave error in judgement. He pulled his heavy leather jacket off and laid it across the saddle. Wiley met him to take his horse into the barn to be fed a flake of hay, brushed, and watered.

The chilling West Texas wind of late December cooled the prickly tension of anticipation this place always insighted. He reminded himself of the reason for this vexing detour. It was to give Lizzy a final goodbye.

"Mista Brandts, if you ain't a sight fo sore eyes! I figured it wus 'bout time fer ya to be wanderin' in purty soon. Do Miss 'lizbeth know yor back from up noth? No, s'pect she don't, but she will d'rectly."

Will grimaced at Wiley's inside knowledge of his habits, but he smiled amiably and shook the black man's hand. He liked Wiley and felt sorry for his lot in life. Politics and the nature of this place trapped him here, but he had nowhere else to go.

"Wiley, it's sure good ta see ya too! Take extra good care of my horse for me. He's tha best one I got!"

Wylie beamed, "Sure, Suh, ya knows I a'ways do! I takes extry good care a yer ho'se, Mista Brandt. Go on in, bet by now Miss 'lizbeth surely knows y're here. This house has a fas' way a gettin' tha w'rd 'roun' betta than the Pres'dent!"

Bidding him farewell, Willheim promised to visit later. He knew Wylie wanted to hear about his travels. The elderly man never ventured off this place.

Will took the steep front steps two at a time and banged the knocker on the door. It opened before the last knock with Nadine Welch standing in the threshold looking like the cat who'd swallowed the canary.

"Why, it's Will Brandt, about time you darkened this door again. Elizabeth isn't going to wait around on you forever, you know. Get yourself in here! I'll buy you a double whiskey and give you a smoke on the house! You know you're in the finest house of business south of the Red River and north of the Rio Grande!"

The tough old red head met him eye to eye as she spoke. There was no doubt she had the brass to go up against any man. Her starchy countenance made men think twice before going up against her. She was one brave female especially with the double-barreled shotgun Will knew she kept under the counter.

His little sister, Katrina, had much the same attitude except for a few defining differences. Baby Sister didn't make a living pedaling women! Kat earned her money honestly by roaming the western prairies, taking photographs, and writing stories for big newspapers back east, and she could stand up for herself with or without a gun! He'd put his money down on Sis any day of the week.

Nadine was stalling and deliberately keeping him waiting to see Lizzy. He turned down both the whiskey and the cigar. His patience was getting thin. She droned on about the weather, news in Sweetwater and Abilene, and her turnover in staff.

He gritted his teeth and tightened his jaw. If she dared mention Tavy being a horse thief or his suicide, he'd yank her out from behind the bar by the dyed hair on her head and shake her like a ragdoll!

Nadine's rapid-fire chatter let up abruptly, and she threw her head back laughing ludicrously.

"Guess you'd like to see one of my girls this afternoon. It's too early yet, you know, but for a steady customer, Mr. Brandt, I'll make an exception. You've been on the trail a mighty long time. The hankering for a warm, soft girl to bed must be powerful…mmm?

"Should I call a few of my best beauties down for you to pick the one you'd like? I've hired some new girls since you were last here. I'm wondering who might tickle your fancy, or better yet, could you handle two this time?"

He was steaming mad by now and red in the face. The lascivious question struck a nerve. The truth was he had come to see Elizabeth to right a wrong, and this witch was reminding him he would be expected to pay the price if he wanted time with her! The many dollars the house had collected from him should have curdled his stomach long ago!

He raised his voice causing her to flinch and take one step back, "Enough!".

Pronouncing each word distinctly, through gritted teeth, he seethed.

"Oh, you know exactly whom I'm here to see, Woman! I'm going to see her immediately if I have to go upstairs to find her!"

"You won't have to wait any longer," Nadine said smugly. "I know the only girl you're wanting. She is waiting in the piano room for you right now, Willheim.

"You're ruining my business, you know. My Lizzy is in love with you. My prettiest girl on the floor, and she has no enthusiasm to earn money for me with any customer but you. Marry her with my blessings, Cowboy. Make an honest woman of her for the love of God. I need her room!

"I'm weary of you showing up on my doorstep!"

Nadine's taunting words both stung and infuriated him. He glared at her with his fists balled up tight at his thighs. Finally, he turned and took his leave.

~*Nadine Welch*

Measured by his snapping words, something had changed in Mr. Willheim Brandt. She'd seen something like this play out in one or two other clients. This cowboy was restless and unhappy with this business arrangement. He might or might not come back to her place again. On the other hand, he could very well be here to offer Elizabeth a marriage proposal.

She figured today's visit could go either way. For Elizabeth's sake, she hoped beyond all hope Brandt came here with a proposal in mind. Maybe he'd take her home today to old Martin Brandt's house for Christmas.

Òh, wouldn't it be something?

~*Will Brandt*

Suddenly Willheim had taken an absolute loathing to everything about this place. It was as if a curtain had been pushed back, and he was seeing everything clearly for the first time. If Nadine Welch was a man instead of imitating one, he would have thrown a solid punch to her jaw!

Instead, he exited the foyer and made his way to the burgundy-colored room with the big grand piano. He hadn't even bothered to pay. Let the old birdie wait for her dirty money. This was one time the high and mighty Madam could wait until he was ready to leave!

Without knocking, he pushed open the heavy door, and there stood Elizabeth Hartley dressed in the whitest lingerie and looking like an angel. The lightest, laciest fabric draped her gorgeous body and left nothing to his imagination.

The two lovers stood silent, as if under a spell. He was soaking up every detail, and if possible, she was even more gorgeous than he remembered.

Dark, auburn curls framed her porcelain face. It curled around her tiny shoulders with some locks tumbling down to touch her breast. The rest was no doubt a wide waterfall all the way to her waste in the back. Her breasts were the size of big, ripe apples. Blushing nipples pointed with arousal and were visible under the sheer cloth. Her small waist flowed downward to full, womanly hips. The contours of her slender legs could be tracked upward to the V visible beneath the gown.

She had evolved into a woman this year. Willheim didn't see a pretty girl but a stunning siren for whom he had not prepared himself. His self-control was being tested, the sleeping brute inside of him roared to life.

Chapter 9

The Cameo

~*Elizabeth Hartley*

Elizabeth had plans for this cowboy standing before her. The enlarged proof of his interest was evidence of the power she wielded over him. It brought Will Brandt back to her bed every time. Keeping a man hooked had less to do with love and more to do with the ache of his lust. Lizzy had skills guaranteed to wind this one up.

He was her most anticipated, repeat customer, and she had been expecting him to arrive for days. She planned to become Mrs. Willheim Brandt sooner rather than later. The time was at hand to lasso this cowboy and reel him in! Elizabeth was a seductive female who knew how to use her womanly wiles to seal the deal whenever she was ready.

Perhaps if she had stopped to think, she might have detected something amiss. Today, he came minus some important tells such as his lack of laughter, sparkless eyes, and the absence of the teasing arch of an eyebrow. Elizabeth's over-confidence and selfishness blinded her, and these little details totally escaped her.

She saw him only as a sex deprived cowboy who had

returned to her bosom because of the delicious triggers he craved. It was so easy to use his own on basic hunger against him. She'd been treading water long enough.

She had always considered him to be a commodity at her disposal. Her affections had nothing to do with what was good for him. The greedy bitch had always been in control. Does a black widow give one whit about a fly's freedom?

She was ready to swim, and the adulteress within grew impatient. She made the first move in this standoff. With a sugary-sweet smile, she sprinted across the space between them with remarkable speed and launched herself into the air. She left him with no choice but to catch her up into the embrace of his thick muscled arms lest she fall.

She knew he wouldn't allow her to hit the hardwood floor. Though he'd never put his love for her into words, she was sure the arms wrapped securely around her meant he was enamored. She had planned from the very beginning for him to be her golden ticket out of this house. She was as good as gone.

It was no secret he came from a well-heeled family in the area, and she planned to marry into the clan all along. She would ride Will's coattails beyond the perimeters of The House of Satin and go to where her life wasn't controlled by the old, outdated madam.

How convenient this was her first day back on the floor after suffering the monthly complaint. She had yet to entertain a visitor, and it seemed fortuitous Will would be the first. The timing couldn't have been better!

In her grandiose delusions, she was absolutely certain he would ask her to be his bride on this trip home. She would never be bought and tumbled by another disgusting, twisted customer ever again! She truly hated men which was a bit ironic!

~*Will Brandt*

The physical urges of a man's body work against his resolve, and her brazen display of lewd behavior broke through his determination to only say what he had come to say and leave. His mind betrayed him and overrode his good sense. From past experiences with this woman, desire bloomed in anticipation of touching her soft naked skin again. His blood heated and his jeans tightened as they had always done before.

The primitive need for relief kept building until his preconceived intentions vaporized. Lizzy had literally thrown herself at him. What was a man to do? She had extended an open invitation to do all the lusty things he shouldn't. Every one of his nerve endings was firing and his well-intended will power had disappeared.

It was too late to turn down her offer now. Seeing and feeling her firm, curvy body in his arms drove him like a wild animal. He'd gone without a woman's soft charms for far too long. Her beauty and willingness to give herself to him were his undoing, and he was too weak to stop.

Knowing full-well he would regret this later, he carried the temptress, none too gently, up the back staircase. He bounded two steps at a time to quickly enter and slam the door of her bedroom shut. They both began stripping off each other's clothes in haste and fell onto the featherbed.

Without talk, finesse, or foreplay, the two collided in a fevered, boisterous, and almost painful coupling. The total act was done and over in but a mere moment. Beethoven could not have written a more stormy or succinct piece of music. The sharp eighth notes built to a crescendo and an explosive climax ripped through them both at the same time.

Once spent, Will jerked himself apart from her. He knew their last tune together had forever been played.

With a pouty, lower lip she begged for his continued attention. Now, the pretense of desire she performed for his benefit had no effect on him whatsoever. He averted his eyes away from her sitting up in the bed on full display. Big teary drops rolled down her cheeks.

Will felt nothing but disgust for himself and her. He was a customer no different from the others she serviced. This was just a job. He sure got his money's worth and would pay for it on the way out the front door.

He pulled his jeans on and was tucking in his shirt. He concentrated on buttoning his pants and securing his heavy gun belt into place after he got his boots back on his feet. These chores were the sobering anchors he needed for his heart to return to a normal rhythm.

"What are you doing, Will? You're not going, are you?" Elizabeth snuffled along with syrupy pleas as she pulled on the fabric of his clothing coaxing him to sit down beside her. He resisted and gave no answers.

"Will, Baby, I'll have the cook bring up a supper tray with all your favorites. We'll stay together all night, right here, just you and me, Baby. We'll take a warm, soaking bath together later. Nadine won't expect me to return to the floor as long as you're here, Honey.

"You're the only one tonight and even forever if you want, Will," she added in a timid, submissive voice.

Finally, Elizabeth looked up into his unresponsive, unsmiling face. The missing smile she had overlooked on his face before caused her breath to hitch.

Still, he said nothing.

She panicked and resorted to the old familiar game they played every year when he returned from the trail.

"What did you bring me for Christmas, Will? Let me see it! Where is it? Give it to me, I can't wait, Sugar."

She tilted her head back, batted her lashes, and twisted a lock of thick hair demurely around her index finger and nibbled her bottom lip.

Will knew he had been overly cruel and had used her badly this afternoon. It was the first time he had ever taken advantage of her. The guilt and shame he felt made him silently curse himself. He should have put an end to this charade long before it got this far. He should not have ignored his original intentions.

This was an affair which never should have been. A gift seemed lame. It couldn't come close to making up for his cold deliberate treatment of Lizzy. Halfheartedly, he decided to play along and give her the red velvet bag. It would be a departing gift. There was an exquisite cameo necklace inside. He had bought it for her in one of the towns he had passed through.

"I didn't know you wanted anything, Elizabeth. Besides, there were few stores along the trail I rode."

"Aw Will! Surely, I know you're teasin' me, now. You did bring me something, didn't you, just a little something, Will?" she persisted, using baby-talk to elicit his attention.

"Let me see. Now, where'd I put it? Give me a minute ta think."

She lay back on the bed alluringly and watched him closely.

He fumbled around in the pockets of his new britches and finally pulled out the red velvet bag secured by a shiny, black satin ribbon. Without touching her, he dropped it between her delicate, still exposed breasts.

"Here you go, Liz. This is for you. It's pretty like you are."

Quickly, she sat up causing the pouch to slip onto the bed. She grabbed it and pulled one end of the ribbon releasing the opening of the sack. She emptied its contents into her palm.

A cameo of the rarest beauty, set in a golden bezel, and hanging from a golden chain spilled into the cup of her hand. An elegant woman's cream-colored image had been carved into the cameo shell. It showed creamy against the rich, caramel-colored background.

Elizabeth squealed like a child in delight.

"Oh, it's gorgeous! Put it on me, now, Darlin', please. I've never gotten such an expensive gift!"

Not bothering to hide her nakedness with the sheet, she sat cross-legged on the bed and waited for him to comply. Truly, Will's heart wasn't in it, but he fastened the clasp. Seeing it around her slender throat made him regret he'd given it to her. It was a present fit for a smitten man's bride, not a prostitute.

It was the only thing Elizabeth wore now, and he took one last look at the cameo resting against her skin. Standing beside the bed, looking down, he couldn't help but feel pity for Elizabeth Hartley, but what could he do? He was only one of many dozen who had lain with her in this very bed. They all paid to do the same act he'd just completed.

Willheim knew he owed it to her to be straightforward before leaving. He could not ride off into the sunset and have her wondering if he was coming back.

"Elizabeth, I've been thinking about this for a while. Trail life isn't as appealing as it used to be. I've grown tired of it. After Mama's passing last year, I had a hard time riding off and leaving Pa.

"The yearning in his eyes for me to stay home, why it near broke my heart. It caused me to consider settling down in Sweetwater this spring, and I won't be leaving again."

"Yes, Will," she whispered.

"I rode all the way back here, thinking of seeing you again and weighing my loyalties between you and my kin. I made a decision once and for all. I owe it to my family and the children I aim to have to be true to them and my upbringing."

Willheim Brandt's words sounded like he was working up a proposal! Dreams might finally come true for her. Any wife of his could shop in Sweetwater with her head held high. She could go into his sister's store instead of traveling out of town to make purchases. No longer would she have to hide from the people of Sweetwater.

"Oh, Will! Oh!" She breathed deeply, visibly trembling. "What are you saying?"

"I'm saying you deserve to know I won't be coming here to see you again, I'm sorry it has to be this way.

"Our arrangement is not my future. I can't marry someone in your profession. Start looking for a man who can. You should be happy."

She sucked in a long, loud breath and let it out just as hard. Tears spilled rapidly down her cheeks and dripped off her face. The salty water landed on her breasts in drops making them glisten.

"I'm sorry I have to be so blunt, but I won't keep stringing you along. I'm tired of following the trail and am serious about starting a family.

"We've had a whole lot of fun together as friends, but the reality is we both need to move on with our lives separately. I'm sorry if I've disappointed you."

The room became deathly silent. Her stare was blankly surreal. It dawned on him he needed to get out, quickly. He wished she'd say something, but she continued to stare past him at the wall like she didn't even remember he was there.

She pulled the pendant until a link in the chain broke. The cameo was clasped so tightly in her fist, her fingers and knuckles became translucent for the lack of blood flow. It was a mistake to have given her the exquisite cameo at the last minute. He had sought to soften the blow of saying goodbye, but it hadn't softened anything.

Suddenly, he was desperate to get out of her room. He abruptly turned his back on the ghostly-looking woman frozen in shock.

He ran down the stairs faster than he'd carried her up. He was anxious to clear the outside door of The House of Satin and breathe the crisp, winter air once again. He couldn't wait to forget this place and put it behind him.

As he barreled by Nadine's counter, he carelessly threw five gold coins down. They clattered and slid against the polished wood. A couple of the coins landing and rolling on the floor as he slammed the door shut behind him. These were sounds he remembered for a long time!

Chapter 10

A Woman Scorned

~Elizabeth Hartley

Blindsided, insulted, and feeling more lowdown than a whipped dog didn't even begin to describe the effect Will's verbal rejection had cast on Elizabeth. How dare he have the nerve to think he could abandon her! No one left Elizabeth Hartley until she was ready.

She had him wrapped around her little finger. He danced to the tune of her fiddle. This cowboy had no future separate from hers. She would be Willheim's bride! She'd belong to the respected Brandt family yet. It was her decision to make. It had never been his decision!

When did everything go so wrong? How did I let him slip through my fingers?

He'd been dallying with her and no one else in this house for years. He always came back to her, but today he made her feel dirty and thrown away like trash. Overwhelming Anxiety overcame her and breathing in and out became an erratic struggle.

Of course he could leave her behind. First Ma and Pa left her and now Willheim Brandt was gone. Well, this wasn't the end of it. Her life lay before her in ruins right now, but she'd regroup stronger than ever and get him back. She'd find a new path intersecting with his!

When he was standing at the foot of her bed fully dressed, Elizabeth smelled a rat. She glimpsed a man who'd found his spine at last. There was no hint of the empty passion she'd carefully planted and nurtured between them. Then he walked out, and she was once again stranded alone in the world. The beautiful, self-loving, confident Lizzy was shattered.

Friends! Had her handsome, sexy lover called them friends? The superior cameo with the broken chain was lying on the floor. It was more than a man would give to a friend. It was the perfect gift a lover might give his fiancé, so why did he fasten it around her neck? His absence of emotion depleted her conceived self-worth down to zero.

It was no secret Will paid Nadine to have time with her. The monetary exchange was par and course for The House of Satin. This was a bordello after all, but she had never thought of the business arrangement between Will and the establishment as significant. Now, she understood completely! The money he paid to visit her had always been the crux of their relationship.

He advised her to find someone else to marry! He might as well have said she wasn't good enough for him to marry, bear his children, or to build a future together.

Damn him! Damn him to hell!

I'll figure out a way to put a curse on Willheim Brandt. I will seek my revenge for his slight if it's the last thing I do!

~*Madam Nadine Welch*

Nadine flinched when she heard the bedroom door upstairs slam! The loud, heavy boot stomps coming down the staircase were a bad omen. Willheim was the only man in the house, so she knew it was him. He'd only been here about an hour, which was an unusually short session for him. Apparently, things hadn't gone well.

Brandt didn't look at her or say nary a word. The clatter of the coins hitting wood caused her eyebrows to raise, not in question but in dread of the aftermath ahead. In view of his hurried escape, she thought better of voicing a mouthy sarcasm. As soon as he banged the door so hard it rattled, she rushed upstairs to pick up the pieces.

Something major had just happened to drastically affect the cowboy's parting behavior. She had to find out what caused such a demonstrative display. No doubt, Elizabeth caused his angst, but what had she done?

Nadine feared she knew the scenario without hearing it. There were only two ways this relationship was destined to end from the beginning. From what she had just witnessed, their encounter hadn't boded well for the happily ever after version of a fairytale.

Chapter 11

Merry Christmas!

If horses could sprout wings, Willheim would have demanded his horse to fly above and beyond the dark shadow cast by this wicked house of prostitution. This afternoon had taken a dark turn. Once inside its confining walls his good intentions had morphed into shortsighted, carnal actions. He'd planned only to talk with Elizabeth, but the blatant display of her charms had overridden his trail-weakened body.

Angry with himself, Will had run through the front door like a bat out of hell and immediately started saddling his own horse. He didn't make small talk with Wiley but tossed a plug of chewing tobacco to him instead.

The temperature had dropped significantly when a cold front moved in from the north, and the sky had grown considerably darker. In his urgency to get away, he hadn't bothered to put on his heavy coat against the threatening storm. Willheim took off in a cloud of dust and never once looked back.

Well, this has been one hell of a day!

By the time he'd collected his other horses and gear from town, the wind had picked up even more and carried icy moisture along with it. He could smell snow coming from behind this front and bundled up accordingly.

The man and his beasts breathed the biting winter chill in through their nostrils and exhaled visible clouds of heated breath. His heart was beating as fast as the hooves of the horses met the ground. He was pushing them to gallop southward toward home. His mind was burdened with the recollections of the news about Tavy.

What would Pa think if he showed up with such a loose woman on his arm? Word of her reputation would get back to him sooner rather than later. Even if Pa overlooked it, Will knew he could not. All the men who paid her for entertainment would haunt Will.

What would his answer be like one day if his children asked where he'd met their mother? He locked all thoughts of Lizzy behind him.

Let it go cowboy, let it go. It's all over and done now. Put this mistake forever out of your mind and never repeat it.

Willheim still had no idea what to make of the scruffy message in his pocket. His gut had told him from the beginning his brother wasn't really dead, but he needed more proof than this message. He dang sure knew Tavy wasn't a horse thief, and he wouldn't have ended his own life either!

Wouldn't he know if his brother was dead? Something just wasn't right, but it surely was a mystery!

He was eager to be surrounded by his people. Stepping back into his home would make it easier to think. All of them could put their heads together. They could get to the bottom of Tavy's whereabouts.

He slowed down and rode at a steady pace now. There was no need to keep pushing the horses and taking his personal anxieties out on them. The time he'd lose by slowing the pace would give him the chance he needed to settle his thoughts.

The dogs didn't even run out to greet him with welcoming yips and yaps until he'd almost cleared the gate. Sure enough, Blacksmith had a big, red Christmas ribbon tied around his neck! All three of his dogs had been rubbed down, combed, and clipped until their coats were shiny and sleek. It was easy to see the kids had given them royal treatment.

Adults and children boiled out of the house in a disorganized ruckus full of greetings. The riot of hugs, questions, and laughter was enough to make all but Rope Tail shy away. There was his father standing on the wrap around porch in his wool stockinged feet observing the family. He leaned on the old cane brought all the way over on a ship from Germany by a grandfather.

Words weren't really necessary between Pa and his youngest son. Their eyes locked, and they simply nodded to one another. Will didn't miss the glimmer of wetness betraying how glad the old man was to have him home.

After the initial hullabaloo was quiet, he searched for Kat in the crowd and easily found her. Little Katrina, who was really not so small anymore, would forever be the baby sister in this clan. He, Tavy, and Kat had spent a lot of time together growing up.

Tavy and Mama were absent from this joyous homecoming, and they left a big hole in the family.

Nickolas and his children offered to take care of the horses. The kids quarreled about who would lead the two-colored mare. Then came the question, "What is her name, Uncle Will?"

"This little beauty belongs to you children and your daddy. I can't rightly introduce you proper-like because she doesn't have a name yet!"

A chorus of jubilee went up among the kids. "Pa, Pa, can we name the horse, please, please, please?"

Nick grinned and nodded.

"Well, a filly this pretty deserves to be called something if she's gonna stay around here. I guess you kids better pick a name, because I don't have the time for it today. All of you have to agree on what to call her though. Do you understood what I'm saying?"

"Yes, Sir! We will." They all said at once.

Will laughed when his brother-in-law winked at him.

The youngsters crowed in smothering their new mare with hugs, pets, and love. The little horse would have a good life here on the farm. She'd be well fed, get lots of attention, and be content. He'd put money down betting she'd have a braided tail and a ribbon to wear when everyone went out on Christmas Eve morning to cut a cedar tree to be decorated in the evening.

Meta Anna hollered for them to end the fracas and put all the horses into the big paddock to graze. She announced supper would be on the table directly. It sounded like something Matilda Brandt would have said.

Meta Anna had cooked a great feast like their ma would have too. The table and kitchen counter were loaded with ham, sweet potatoes, canned vegetables from last summer's garden, cornbread, black coffee, lemonade, and enough minced meat pies with thick cream to feed them all.

While she and Kat rushed around to get the meal finished and set out on the long harvest table, the noise level increased. Martin Brandt sat calmly in his easy chair, taking the hubbub all in with a small smile. It was a blissful occasion for him to have most of the family under one roof again.

No one was ignoring Tavy's absence, but there would be no sad talk of him in front of the children today. What was done was done and hashing it all out could wait until later.

The noisy chaos of everyone talking at once became silent in honor of Meta Anna who preserved the heritage and kept alive the loving Brandts' closely-knit traditions. She was the family's keeper of the home fire. This being December 23, the night before Christmas Eve, she'd set the table as if for a grand party. The same dishes their dear mother would have used were filled with similar foods she would have made.

Tonight, most of the clan, including the children, gathered around the long harvest table to break bread together. Savannah Grace's family would join them tomorrow evening for a light supper, refreshments, and the trimming of the tree. There would be a few tears as they recalled the many past Christmas seasons.

How thankful everyone was to Nick and Meta Anna for holding the home together for them! Mateas, called to be an evangelist, offered a fine prayer in his rich mahogany voice. He thanked God for the great bounty set before them and for this home place He preserved for them. In his prayer were tributes in honor of their missing brother, Tavias, and their loving mother, Matilda.

With everyone gathered at the table, Mateas closed his words with an Amen in Jesus's name. Soon after, a great clatter of plates and silverware, laughter, and talk arose. The volume was back up to where it had been left off. This was Christmas, and it carried on with a great deal of happiness and optimism.

As usual and customary at any other meal, their father ate rather quickly and removed himself from the table to smoke his pipe. He scraped back his wooden chair and retired to his overstuffed one in the parlor.

No one thought anything about him leaving the table early. He was content to listen as his family visited and carried on with the party. When the pies and cream were served, one of the children took a thick wedge of it and a mug of coffee to him.

After the meal was eaten and everyone was engorged from overindulgence, it was left to the women to tidy up the mess. The children were sent upstairs still chattering about the sweet, two-colored mare Uncle Will brought them today and listing good names for her.

They were looking forward to cutting a big cedar in the morning too. They were excited about bringing the decorations down from the attic. Soon no noises, footsteps, or laughter could be heard from their quarters above. They were most likely snuggled between toasty quilts, already dreaming sweet dreams of sugarplums.

Chapter 12

A Plan Is Born

The Brandt brothers and Sister Kat slipped out to check the horses and breathe the open, crisp air they relished. The barn was chilly, but the walls sheltered them from the freezing wind and moisture. Heavy coats, gloves, and wool scarves made being outside the house tolerable.

Age was beginning to show in the lines around Morgan's eyes, and he didn't step quite as lively as he had in the past. He was the eldest son and had more years under his belt than any of them when it came to roaming the tall grass prairie. It wasn't surprising to hear him talk of marrying the widow, Letty Taylor, and settling down.

She owned a farm and a tightly built ranch house close to Sweetwater. The widow was raising two growing boys and a girl by herself. With one dependable, hired hand and industrious children helping, Letty continued to live on the farm and survive off its earnings.

The income she made was good enough, but it was a hard row to hoe for a woman alone. Morgan was sweet on her, and the two were well-suited. They both needed the close relationship marriage offered. Morgan farming beside her, helping to raise the children, and perhaps having a baby of their own would be ideal. Morgan was ready to take a wife and have a family. In the spring, they intended to tie the knot.

Mateas was called to preach God's Holy Word when he was very young. He had been riding the trails not just as a cowboy but also as an evangelist. He dedicated his life to serving the Lord in thoughts, words, and deeds. Now, he yearned to pastor his own congregation and settle down in one place.

The colored settlement near Walnut Grove was growing, and Mateas had been evangelizing there. The people were building a small church and parsonage and had officially asked him to be their preacher.

Kat had no specific plans except to continue writing, sketching, and taking pictures for the big newspapers back east. This past year, the publications bought anything she sent and begged her for more. The readers' appetites were voracious for anything depicting life in the wild west.

She aimed to take advantage of this hunger by continuing to follow the herds, see the ranches and homesteads, and visiting cattle towns for a while longer. Most women didn't venture out unescorted, but Katrina was self-sufficient, tough as nails, and wise as an owl.

Will listened with interest to all of them but didn't mention he was done pushing cattle and planned not to go back. They'd find out later he was going to stay here, build a house, marry, and start a family. News of Tavy's mysterious death had put thoughts of his own future on the back burner for the time being. Until all of the facts were known, Will wouldn't be satisfied.

Morgan, the unappointed leader, was the first to make mention of Tavy this evening. Of course, their brother's absence weighed heavily on all their minds, but this was the first opportunity to talk about it in private.

"Pa has decided to send us to Adobe Wall the day after Christmas. He wants Tavy's body brought back home and laid to rest with Ma. I reckon he's right on it."

There was nodding and mumbling in agreement.

"Be ready ta leave tha day after Christmas before daylight. We're gonna take a look-see in the panhandle 'n' ask questions 'til we git answers. Pa needs ta know what happened at Adobe Wall. Well, I 'magine we all need ta know what really happened ta Tavy. Papa's not sa sure 'bout what Sweetwater's sheriff wus tol' to tell 'im."

Everyone in the barn murmured again in agreement. Will took this as the opportune time to bring up the dirty envelope he found waiting for him at the Post Office. It was burning a hole in his shirt pocket. He held off showing it to his brothers because he didn't want Papa getting wind of it yet when they didn't know anything for sure.

Willheim cleared his throat decisively, and everyone in the barn turned to look at him.

"When I made it to Sweetwater today, I heard the tale circulatin' 'bout Tavy. Then I discovered this curious envelope waitin' in my General Delivery pile."

They all froze, stone-still, and waited on alert as he pulled the folded envelope from his shirt pocket.

"It's postmarked, Albuquerque, Texas 'n' dated from a few weeks back. Tha writing on tha front is scrawled like a child wrote it. It's strange but not as disturbing as tha scrap of pasteboard inside with curious words scratched into it from Tavias. At least it looks ta be a message from our brother, but I can't make any sense of it a'tal.

"Tha envelope is addressed to me, but I figure it was meant fer us all. There has ta be a hidden meaning ta these few words. We've got ta put our heads tagether 'n' figure out what he might have been tryin' ta tell us."

They gathered closer around the flickering light cast by the two hanging lanterns. The envelope and pasteboard were passed around for each to study. Finally, Will commenced to talk again.

"Ya'll know how close I am ta Tavy. When Savannah told me what had happened taday, it hit me like a cannon ball in tha gut. I couldn't come to terms with any part a tha story she had to tell. Deep down I felt a chance Tavy was still alive, but how could he be after what the sheriff told Papa? Where could he be?

"Wouldn't I feel it in my heart if he was dead? Unless I kin find out fer sure what happened, I refuse ta believe Tavy's gone."

Everybody commenced talking at once until Morgan demanded they stop. He spoke up to the group huddled together in the barn.

"Papa expects us ta go to Adobe Wall. I suggest we do what he wants. We'll go ta tha Panhandle and see if we kin find Tavy's body. If we do, then we'll know he's dead fer sure. Then, we'll stay there 'til we get ta tha bottom a what happened 'fore we come back here.

"But, if we don't find a body er don't like tha answers we git, I say, we ride ta Albuquerque 'n' look fer our brother there. It's the only other lead we have. I'm like you, Will, there's somethin' not right 'bout any a this. There's got ta be more to tha story!

"Does anyone have anything ta add?"

All of them shook their heads in unison and murmured in agreement with Morgan.

"Good! Git yer gear together. Pack plenty a ammunition in case we run into trouble. I'll tell Papa when we're leaving."

Chapter 13

Christmas Eve

After a bowl of oatmeal, bacon, and buttered biscuits breakfast the next morning, the whole family bundled up and headed to the southwest range where the cedars grew best. This is where they go every year to cut down a special tree for the Christmas Eve party. Meta Anna was riding on the wagon seat tucked in between Nick and Papa.

Just like Will had figured, the children had braided red and green ribbons into the two-colored horse's white mane and tail. Silver bells were attached to her bridle and ringing gayly with every step. All three of the Austin children sat atop their new pet all in a row. They decided to name her Merry Christmas Eve. The mare gayly carried the gaggle of children on her back. She'd found a good home here on the farm.

The brush dogs kept pace alongside Eve and the kids. Laughing children, wiggly dogs, and a sweet-natured pony were a joy for the adults to watch. The cowboys on their seasoned horses and the wagon bearing a green wreath for decoration moved along in sync leaving their mark on the snow sprinkled prairie. A path of flattened grass stretched out behind the family's traditional holiday parade.

Once the tree had been chosen, cut, and loaded onto the wagon, the procession turned around and retraced their trail back home. Mateas started singing Christmas carols honoring the birth of baby Jesus. Everyone was smiling and eager to join the choir!

Nick and Morgan nailed the cedar onto a stand before taking it into the house. It stood imposingly in the family room just off the kitchen where it would sit for the rest of the day undecorated. As the tree warmed, the fragrant cedar scent filled the room like a festive perfume.

Aunt Katrina popped three large buckets full of homegrown popcorn. The toasty aroma of the corn mingled with the smells of the cedar, peppermint candy canes, freshly baked cookies, cinnamon apple cider, fresh loaves of hot bread, and the sweet syrup ready to form popcorn balls!

The general store in Sweetwater had closed early this afternoon, and Savannah's family joined everyone as soon as they could lock the door and get away! All the children sat on the floor in a circle stringing ropes of white popcorn to drape on the cedar tree. The men scrubbed their hands and made quick work of forming popcorn balls to hang from the boughs with colored twine Ely had brought from the store.

The women scurried around assembling platters of sandwiches, meat hand pies, pickles, jams, cookies, sweet rolls, tiny cakes, nuts, and homemade candies. Savannah made their traditional pink punch with the ingredients she'd brought with her.

Kat stirred a pot of hot chocolate from the afternoon milking, carefully stirring so the liquid wouldn't scorch. Apple cider was kept warm on the stove. Nothing ever smelled as tempting as the decorating party on Christmas Eve.

The children and the men decorated the tree using a ladder to top it with a shiny, yellow, tinfoil star. Bright red glass balls brought from Germany years ago and white paper angels made by the children were hung on the branches. This was one time snacking all evening was encouraged.

Ely, Savannah Grace, and their children would sleep over to join in the fun of being part of the big family. Before bedtime, Mataus read the true Christmas story from the Book of John, and other secular storybooks were read. Then, just before bedtime the kids hung their stockings on the mantle in hopes Old St. Nick would fill them while they slept.

Some of the men had gone hunting for wild turkey yesterday. The two birds and a ham from the smoke house would be baked in the woodstove in the morning for tomorrow's Christmas Day feast!

Chapter 14

Caught Between Two Rocks

~*Tavias Brandt*

Tavias Brandt had been caught in an ambush along with Elijah and Winston Saxton, his soon-to-be-brothers-in-law. They had barely made it to cover in time, but their problems were far from over based on the racket and insults coming from outside.

They were pinned down in a small space. They were quite literally trapped like animals with no foreseeable options except for one which would probably result in their deaths. Tavy didn't have much prospect of getting them out of this structure unharmed.

The front side where they entered the space was splintery, gray, weathered wood. It was dry and rickety. A door hanging cockeyed by a lone rusting hinge attached at the bottom was the only way in and the only way out. Tavy had dragged it shut and loosely secured it with a piece of rusted wire to hold it in place.

The saving grace was the fact the wooden wall with

the cock-eyed door was wedged between two adjacent walls of solid rock meeting in the middle at the back forming a triangle. A natural overhang formed the roof. A rough rectangle cut into the wood served as a window. Rays of light showed through it and around the sides of the loosely fitting door.

Tavy recognized this was a deathtrap when he ran inside, but there had been no other choice to make under the desperate circumstances. He and the Saxton brothers had gone out early this morning to hunt wild game to roast for the wedding. The reason for the outing was forgotten as bullets peppered them. Tavias and his party were no longer hunters. They were now the prey being hunted.

Tavy was smitten by a golden-haired girl who lived near San Antoine in the back country of Gonzales County. Elijah and Winston were two of her several brothers. He was staying in their family's barn in the scrubby, socially backward, wilderness of the South Texas hills.

He had no knowledge of the hill people's culture and realized too late it was mostly about feuding and fighting. The Saxton clan was constantly quarrelling with the Butler clan. The volatile clash had been going on for decades, and no one even remembered what had started it. Tavy was not prepared for the cruelty the hill people were capable of inflicting on each other out of purely, ignorant hatred.

By association, he found himself automatically counted on the side of the Saxton Clan because he and Valentine Saxton were courting. Tavy was dismayed when he realized the dangerous, festering resentment between the two groups of clansmen.

He had decided it was best to get Valentine and himself out of these hills as soon as possible. These uneducated and isolated people were hell bent on causing pain and killing each other! Tavy planned to take his bride and start to Sweetwater the day after the wedding. As far as he could discern, the only times the clansmen weren't fighting were during the planting and harvest seasons.

Listening with mounting apprehension to the taunts and shouting of the men outside, he hopelessly put his back to a rock wall and slid down into a sitting position, crossing his arms on his bended knees to make a place to rest his head and pray.

God, where is Willheim? I could sure use his confidence and courage right about now! Please, Father, tell me what to do.

Tavy was literally caught between two rocks and a hard place. Little ammunition was left between Elijah and him.

They were only armed with Elijah's scatter gun, Tavy's Remington rifle, and his Army Colt sidearm. The way Tavy saw it; they could only hold them off for a little while longer. What most worried him was what would become of his sweetheart, Valentine Saxton, if he didn't make it out alive.

Winston was young and handicapped with the chronic simple thinking of a child. He hadn't grasped the dire predicament they were facing. He only had a slingshot but could knock the eyeball out of a sparrow with it if he had a clear shot. His phenomenal skill wasn't helpful at this range against guns. Tavias was not one to throw in the towel in a fight, but he couldn't fathom anything ahead but pending disaster.

It was near the end of November, and the three had gone hunting. There had been no signs of trouble until without warning, it was suddenly upon them. It forced a chaotic dash for cover. They'd been strategically driven to this deathtrap for cover. The evidence of spent shell casings scattered around their feet spoke of other standoffs.

Tavias and Valentine were truly in love. Now, there was a very good chance he'd never see his beautiful girl again. He was afraid for her if he died. The first time they had made sweet love under the stars; he discovered she'd never lain with another man. She was pure as the driven snow., and he was her first. He swore to himself right then he'd marry her and take the angel with golden hair away from these hills and back to Sweetwater with him.

They could have a life of peace, safety, and comfort among the Brandt people and living on their own piece of land. They would raise a houseful of babies in a home he'd build with his own two hands. Now his dreams were fading fast. He could no longer visualize them clearly. There would be no wedding, no babies, and no happy forever after life with his Valentine. But what about his Valentine? Was there still a possible way to set her free from a harsh life among these backward thinking people and their barbaric ways?

Was there even the slightest chance of getting words to Willheim somehow? They were kindred spirits, and he would be the one most likely to understand his passion for Valentine. If anyone could save her it would definitely be Will.

Tavias was caught in the crosshairs of an irrational, moonshine mentality. The Saxtons and Butlers lived on opposite sides of the hills divided by a high ridge, and yet, their addictions to feuding kept them fighting and following their own laws. Ignorantly, they hadn't considered civilization would eventually interfere.

The agitation between the two clans started long before the town of Albuquerque had been established at the southern base of Texas Hill Country. The settlers saw the two clans as white trash and nuisances to be feared. The townships' people were afraid of their crude living, superstitious beliefs, and violent ways.

Harvey Thatcher and William McCorkle, two brothers-in-law who ran the town of Albuquerque, petitioned and pressured the capitol in Austin, Texas for help. They demanded Austin send the Texas Rangers to settle the fighting between the two clans. They wanted an end to the skirmishes, shootings, killings, and unlawful hangings terrifying the territory once and for all.

For many years the Texas government had turned its back and deaf ears to the complaints of feuding in the hills. As more civilized people moved into Gonzales County, dangers of the unchecked feuding became harder to ignore.

A couple of rangers were sent from Austin, Texas on a brief reconnaissance mission to evaluate the problem in Gonzales County. Their findings recommended an officer with a few rangers be sent to root out the trouble and bring the area under civil control so the population below the hills could live without fear.

The Texas Rangers were already spread quite thin at this time with many other problems in the state. Austin elected to send in a harsh regulator, Jack Holt, and his miscreant men to hobble the hill people by any means necessary.

This fallen ranger, known by the name of Holt, was as unconscionable as an outlaw himself, but he was good at dirty work. Holt didn't believe in talking. Instead, his band of thugs ended up injuring and tormenting members of both clans.

He and his henchmen went after them all without discrimination. This brought about a tentative unity of sorts between the two clans and a fragile truce was called. Collectively, they definitely were stronger, and their goal was to rid their hills of the regulator and his men. The hill country peoples often outsmarted Holt and his gang even eventually killing some of them.

It was Holt's renegades who had Tavias and the two Saxtons trapped like sitting ducks. For the last half hour, the men outside had been threatening to set the front of the shack on fire. No doubt, the dry wood would go up in flames like kindling.

Tavy proposed a plan to Elijah. They'd offer to come out if they let his young brother, Winston, get clean away first. Elijah nodded his consent. Together they decided to wait as long as possible before making the deal. It appeared that by the yelled obscenities and the pick-up in bullets spraying the structure, the patience of their enemies was running out.

With resigned regret Tavy called out.

"We'll make ya a deal!"

"Ya'll don't have nothin' we want!" Holt called back, laughing at him.

Tavy yelled back, in an attempt to reason with the man.

"Hear me out! There is a boy with us! The Texas Rangers won't be willing ta look tha other way if ya spill tha blood of a kid. Let 'im get clean away. Once he's safe, we'll walk out 'n' make no more fuss. You'll get back ta camp in time ta eat yer biscuits."

Sweat popped out on Tavy's forehead and dripped off his nose while he waited. Some of the salty perspiration soaked into his eyes and burned. They were stinging, and he kept wiping away the salt water in order to see.

He'd only stuck around in this godforsaken hill country because he was in love with a girl he happened upon in the woods. She was his Valentine. If not for her catching his attention, he'd be back in Sweetwater already and settling in for the winter.

"Yeah, send the boy out! We won't fire on 'im as long as he scoots out fast."

"Give us a minute ta make peace with our maker. I'll tell ya when he's ready ta go."

Taking his right boot off, he tore out a ragged piece of the worn cardboard lining. It wasn't ideal, but it was the only thing he could think of to write something down. Little in this place was of any use and, certainly, there sure was no paper. He found a piece of rusty wire and broke off a shorter piece.

Elijah wasn't paying attention to him or his efforts. He was staring out front through the small window. Death to them both would come soon after Winston was gone and clear away. He and Elijah, both realized it.

It was hard to scratch deep letters into the old, crumbly pasteboard, but Tavy marked it as best he could under the strain of facing his impending fate. He was just so desperate to get word of Valentine to Will. He didn't know what he should say. It was one thing to get himself shot or stretched at the end of a rope but an altogether different thing to desert his innocent, defenseless Valentine here in the middle of a war.

Tavias felt he had to try and get her out, somehow. The one person in the world he had always been able to count on was Willheim. He would never let him down if he needed help. There was an unspoken bond of loyalty connecting the two brothers by an invisible cord. They were not only similar in looks but in the way they took things to heart.

**GET MY
VALENTINE   TAVY**

Taking soot from the remains of a cracked stove, he rubbed it into his etchings making them darker and more visible. He folded the pasteboard and shoved the message into Winston's pocket.

"Boy, I'm countin' on ya to listen. This goes ta my brother. Find someone who can write the address 'n' send it to Will Brandt, Sweetwater, General Delivery. Listen.

"Will Brandt, Sweetwater, General Delivery---Will Brandt, Sweetwater, General Delivery.

"Do ya got it? Say it back ta me."

The nervous boy was able to repeat the instructions back to Will after more repetition. It cost Tavy more patience than his nerves allowed, but Winston finally got it.

Will dug in his pockets and pulled out the money he'd earned on the trail and his gold watch.

"Take this money ta your sister, Valentine. Tell her I

love 'er.

"You can keep the watch for yerself.

"Now, get ready ta run like a deer and don't ya look back until you're all tha way home!"

"Tha boy's coming out!" he yelled. "Don't shoot!"

Looking back at the boy, he said, "Ya run as fast as ya can and swear, you'll get tha paper off ta Will Brandt, Sweetwater, Texas somehow. Don't stop running fer nothin', no matter what ya hear goin' on behind ya."

The frightened boy nodded, and Will shoved him out of the opening. Once freed, he ran like a scalded cat. No immediate shots were fired, and Tavias prayed Will would get his desperate message and come after Valentine.

Elijah and Tavy pitched out their guns. The only thing left to do was go through the doorway and surrender themselves.

"Come out with yer hands in tha air and be quick 'bout it. Don't try nothin'!" The voice snarled.

Valentine's brother, Elijah, not much older than the boy who'd run off, shook hands with Tavy. They looked straight into each other's eyes.

Tavy was scared, but this fear was unspoken. He wondered if he'd see, hear, or feel the bullets first. At least, he hoped for the burn of hot lead instead of being hung. Holt's favorite killing method was done with a rope.

With their hands held high above their heads, the two doomed men walked out with short steps, and Tavy never got the answer to his question, because, mercifully, he blacked out with stabbing pain to his shoulder.

Winston, well away by now, cried out involuntarily with the two shots he heard in the distance behind him. The piece of pasteboard from Tavy's boot was still safely tucked away in his pocket with Valentine's money, and the gold watch. Just to be sure, he felt for them without missing a step. He promised out loud to the God Almighty he would do as Tavy Brandt had asked of him.

Chapter 15

Leaving for Adobe Wall, Texas

Christmas night had turned off extremely cold, and a light sleet was falling before dawn. The Brandts could see their breaths as they saddled the horses in the barn and led them outside. Will's demeanor signaled his dogs there was work to be done. They were antsy to follow their master and Rope Tail on the road again.

The house was still dark and quiet, but Meta Anna had gotten provisions from the kitchen packed last night. The supplies were already in the buckboard. Mateas was driving it to haul Tavy's body home to the family cemetery where Mama was buried.

Papa slid two shovels alongside extra blankets, and sacks of grain for the horses. The shovels were for digging up his son's grave. According to the report from the Sweetwater's sheriff, Tavy was buried way up yonder in the Texas Panhandle.

Mateas would drive the buckboard with his saddle horse tied on back. He was well acquainted with driving wagons long distances. Morgan was on his trail horse,

Willheim on Rope Tail, and Katrina was riding her tall, chestnut stallion, Buckeye. They would follow along in caravan style.

Two hundred miles of winter weather and rugged Texas terrain had to be crossed between here and the Texas Panhandle. It would take several days to reach Adobe Wall. Inclement weather and the buckboard would slow them.

If not for such a sad reason for the trip, it might have seemed like an adventure. The four siblings had not ridden together for some time. The shovels in the back of the wagon were a grim and constant reminder of the task ahead of them.

On the first day, they only pulled over to water and rest the horses a couple of times. They stopped to make a camp along a windbreak in the late afternoon. None of the four were novices to the hardships of riding cross country.

Not a brother, sister, or her papa voiced any qualms about Katrina making the hard journey to Adobe Wall. Kat had proved to her family years ago how tough and skilled she was. She could hold her own as well as any man and better than some.

She had a natural gift for handling horses. Kat had honed her big chestnut, Buckeye, to even the odds while weaving in and around men. The big stallion was trained to help and to keep her safe. He and Katrina were a bonded pair.

Buckeye could run like the wind and stir up a cyclone to avoid trouble. He was handy at positioning himself providing Kat privacy when no shelter was available. He stayed close at night and acted as a sentry alerting her to danger. What a valuable companion for a woman who traveled alone.

Kat could ground tie Buckeye by dropping his reins. She could put two fingers in her mouth and whistle two tones shrilly, and the horse would come find her immediately. One sharp whistle was his signal to buck wildly and throw a rider flat on his back. Buckeye was her ace in the hole on the open range where she took photographs, sketched, and wrote stories to make her living.

Her independence and reputation preceded her by word of mouth around campfires. She was a strong young woman of action, and many had witnessed her and Buckeye work as a team. Katrina Brandt was revered as being wise, careful, observant, and prepared to take care of herself in an ocean of prairie grass, animals, Indians, and cowboys. She was respected and had paid her dues for the right to spread her wings and soar like an eagle.

Mateas was an experienced cowboy and trail cook. Running a chuck wagon was a task he enjoyed. He'd first learned to cook by helping Matilda Brandt in the kitchen when he was growing up. He'd learned the basics and graduated to chuck wagon cook for trail drives.

He'd started out pushing cattle as one of many drovers, but one day after riding drag and breathing the dust of three thousand cattle, he switched jobs. There was some authority in being in charge of the food and doctoring.

A chuck wagon always traveled ahead of the herd and dust to reach the next campsite. Getting a meal started was a peaceful time. The cook also earned as much as ten dollars a month more than a herder!

At the time, he'd been leaning into preaching more and more. A cooking preacher made a great listener and counselor. The combination of his skills was a platform for serving the Lord.

Then there was Will who had witnessed so much. He was seasoned by so many memories, both good and bad. Everyday experiences and situations of life and death had molded him into a tough man.

Losing his friend, Adam Tanner, was one tragedy he would never forget.

Chapter 16

Stampede from the Past

Willheim remembered after he had ridden with Eddy Flores for two years already and Adam Tanner for three, Mateas signed up with Flores's outfit to be the chuck wagon cook. This was the very same year Adam died.

Mateas and Will didn't talk about being brothers, but of course Adam knew because Will didn't keep anything from his good friend. It wasn't common practice for a trail boss to hire brothers or close relatives to work on the same drive.

The practice was frowned upon because all of the men had to be able to trust each other through thick and thin. Matters of life and death could arise, and a man might pick a relative to save first above an acquaintance. Blood was thicker than water, and no one wanted to test it.

Since Mateas was black, and Will was white, their kinship was never questioned by others. Flores knew but hired them both anyway because he considered them to be quality, top hands. The brothers were reliable and had skills. Both were men of integrity and worth their weights in gold.

Adam, died from an accident he suffered during an unforgettable stampede. The catastrophe had broken Will's heart and made an impression on his life forever.

Will remembered everyone had been watching the sky in the west all morning, and he recollected there hadn't been much talking, not like usual. When they rode out after breakfast to get the herd moving, Mateas had told Will later he would always remember how heavy the air felt and how hot and sticky it made his skin.

Mateas said he figured the boys would be extra worn out by suppertime if the humidity kept bearing on them. Before breaking camp and pulling out for the day, he'd put dried peaches in a bucket of water to soak.

For supper, he planned to make peach dumpling cobbler with a meal of chili beans, side meat, and scrambled eggs. A full stomach with an unexpected treat and lively camp music was the best way to loosen up.

Both cowboys and stock were on edge, short-tempered, and jumpy. The stillness of the air, suffocating heat, and the sun's relentless radiation distorted vision. A bank of thunder clouds in the distance threatened. The herd had been restless and hard to manage all day.

It made for a long, tiring day for men and beasts. After eating supper, Sage got out his fiddle and Tailwind joined in on his mouth organ. The reverie was cut entirely too short by Flores who sent all the men back out to watch over the increasingly jittery herd.

Around midnight, a cooler breeze came up, and the wind progressively picked up velocity. The cattle were milling around and making anxious noises. A much cooler drop in temperature happened fast, and a streak of lightning broke the dark sky in half.

The thunder was deafening from the alarming strike. Then cracks of lightning, one after another spread out like tree branches of light followed by rolls of thunder lapped over each other. The steers started churning and could not be calmed.

The long horns of the steers became like lightning rods and arcs eerily jumped between their tips. This phenomenon caused heightened fear among the cattle and the cowboys. The glowing arcs were surreal sights. Panic overtook the beasts, and a frenzy of motion commenced. The noise and confusion were beyond comprehension as the drovers tried to gain control.

Meanwhile Mateas and his young biscuit roller haphazardly speed-broke camp and prepared to get the lifeline of the outfit, the chuck wagon, safe and out of the path of the storm and the cattle's hoofs. If the wagon got run over by a stampede, it would be crushed to smithereens.

Everything, including the cowboys' abandoned bedrolls and other gear was thrown, shoved, and mashed down into the bed of the chuck wagon.

Mateas sent the boy driving away in a fast clip away from any danger of the rig being trampled. The chuck wagon was so important to morale and survival it couldn't be lost.

He shouted over the noise, "Don't stop 'til yer far away. You've got ta keep this rig standin' and safe. I'll catch up later!"

The outfit's wrangler was waiting for the cooky. He had two horses saddled and ready for them to help contain and slow the herd before the animals ran themselves to death. Every available cowboy including these two were needed.

The wrangler had already turned the remaining remuda loose to take care of themselves. Horses were smart and hell bent to get out of the way of trouble. It was their nature to keep themselves safe. They'd end up close enough together to be rounded back up easily later.

Eddy Flores had been out from the beginning and struggling with his men to keep the herd bunched up. At first, the steers milled around like old women, stirring, and blowing indignantly through their nostrils. They made distressed noises from deep in their throats.

The most violent streak of lightning yet ripped down from the sky unexpectantly, and the vibrations of the mighty thunder shook the earth under the animals' hooves. The powerful ground tremor set them off in one hysterically swift movement. The herd was gone as if washed away by an ocean wave. The race was on!

The seasoned cowboys worked as a team and did their best to keep up. They shot guns above their heads trying to redirect the animals. They pushed their horses to their limits and waved their lariats in a unified effort to turn the frightened mass into a counterclockwise circle.

The rain pelted down in stinging drops sounding and torturing exposed skin like jagged hail. The wind blew the torrents into the men's faces and cut visibility close to nothing.

This was along the time Eddy Flores was knocked off his mount and a freaked steer broadsided the horse. Luckily, Adam saw what was happening in an illuminating flash of lightning and came to his rescue. He pulled the boss up under his arm and tightly against the right side of his own horse. It was the best he could do to try and remove him from danger.

Adam was already weakening and didn't have the upper-body strength to pull Flores more than a couple of feet off the ground. It was enough to make a difference. Eddy was stunned by the fall and so addled, he was in a stupor. He could do nothing to help himself.

Will caught a glimpse of the situation in a flicker of light. He saw the boss being precariously dragged along by Adam who was on his own mount. In another revealing flicker, he saw a maverick steer charging toward them both.

The insane brute lowered his head and aimed a long horn for Eddy's back. There was nothing Adam could do to keep him from being gored. Will grasped the dire situation as if time was standing still. In a split second, he made the decision and tracked the prey with his borrowed Colt through the sporadic flashes of vibrating light.

There was no choice but to pull the trigger and shoot blindly into the dark while he and the whole scene was in motion! He begged God to guide his bullet to hit the steer true. There was no time to consider the ramifications of shooting his boss or friend.

Later, he never actually remembered pulling the trigger, but he had remembered the ringing sound of his shot forever. It brought the mad steer down to his knees falling dead in its tracks just inches away from Eddy Flores and Adam! By this time, the herd had submitted to being turned because the steers were winding down in exhaustion, and the storm was losing its punch.

The voracious winds were winding down and continuing more gently across the prairie. The beginning of daylight could be seen peeking along the horizon. There would be strays and the remuda to round up, but the crisis was over, and exhaustion settled into the muscles of the cowboys and animals alike.

They'd layover for a few days to dry out, rest, and let the horses and cattle graze. Amazingly, no person had been killed, but Mateas doctored several injuries. A few horses had been brought down by horns or broken legs, forcing cowboys to put them out of their misery.

As many of the dead steers as possible were butchered. Many steaks would be cooked and eaten. Meat would be cut into strips and dried for jerky and stew meat to cook later. Some of the beef would be salted down.

Will and Adam made it to the chuck wagon which was saved from damage by the cook's boy who was now revered as a hero! Gallons of strong, black coffee, dozens of biscuits, gravy, and as much beefsteak as could be eaten were readily available for the next few days. This recovery time was needed.

Adam had been distracted by fear while rescuing Flores from being trampled to death. It wasn't immediately he realized the little finger of his hand had been ripped clean off sometime during the disaster. The appendage had been sacrificed in the heat of the moment without him even feeling it.

When the enraged steer charged, time had stood still. Had it not been for Will, both boss and friend might be dead. The finger was gone, but until Adam calmed down back in camp no pain called attention to the loss.

Mateas dipped Adam's stump in coal oil and bandaged it. Eddy came around quickly after the ordeal. Both of them were lucky. Adam wouldn't be the only cowboy in the west with a missing finger. It was common enough to catch one between a rope and the saddle horn causing an amputation. No one, even Adam, paid much attention to the injury. It was just one of those times a cowboy had to spit and go on.

Flores was lucky to still be kicking and was indebted to Adam and Will both for saving his life. If Adam hadn't acted so quickly, he would have been a dead man. If Will hadn't come along at the right moment, he would have been gored. They'd saved him from dying twice during the stampede!

"What gun did ya use to shoot the steer, Will?" Eddy asked. "When in the hell did, ya become such a damn good shot? I'm not complaining, mind ya!"

"I used your old hog leg! Don't ya 'member, Eddy? It's the same gun ya loaned me to carry on my first cattle drive.

"I'm sentimental about this gun, Boss. I just never give it back to ya 'cause I'm a right bit superstitious of being without it. I 'spose I should give it back to ya now. It's 'bout time, don't ya think?" Will drawled his words.

He unholstered the handgun and offered it butt first back to its rightful owner and waited for him to reach for it.

Flores held both his palms in the air, shaking his head

and laughing whole-heartedly.

"Just keep it, Ole, Son. I 'b'lieve it's servin' me way better in your holster. I might be needin' ya ta save my life ag'in some time on down tha trail!"

"Mateas, pour a shot 'a whiskey 'round fer every cowpoke on the payroll, including yer young biscuit roller. We've all earned a swig on this night!"

Within a week after the stampede Adam was so sick with fever he couldn't work, and he rode by day in the chuck wagon. Mateas doctored him as best he could, but the injured hand turned morbidly black with the smell of putrefaction all pioneers and cowboys feared. Angry looking stripes inched up his arm, splitting his swollen flesh and oozing green, sticky pus.

There was no other choice but to take his arm off above the elbow. The primitive procedure was no small task. Flores and Will helped Mateas with the nasty task, and thankfully Adam passed out cold. Mateas cauterized the wound with a red-hot knife.

Wrapped in a flour sack, Willheim carried the odorous waste a long distance from the camp and buried it deep in the ground. He never told anyone he had vomited his toenails up and cried like a baby until he had no more tears left.

Mateas doctored Adam as best he could with what he had, and then he preached over his grave as well. Without even telling his brother, Will later sent money and instructions home to Pa to have a marker made bearing the name Adam Tanner and to place it in the Brandt family cemetery. At last Adam had found his family. It was inscribed, A TRUE AND FAITHFUL BROTHER.

CHAPTER 17

TAVY'S GRAVE UNCOVERED

The trip into the Panhandle was hindered by miserable weather. The foursome methodically ate up mile after mile with their heads down bearing up against the bitter cold wind from the north without complaining. The trail they followed was no more than two very faint ruts in the snow broken here and there by tufts of dry grass. This was not a kind season for anyone to be traveling.

The last night spent outside of Adobe Wall; they were huddled closely together around a big, crackling fire establishing their plans. Morgan took the reins, and no one argued with their big brother who had been a well-respected trail boss and had led many drives from Texas all the way up to the Dakotas or into Montana. He had a good head for calling shots and experience and guts backed him up.

It was decided only Will and Kat would enter the settlement of Adobe Wall together before Morgan and Mateas were seen by anyone. The two brothers would leave the wagon hidden and go in separately. Lone men would have a better chance of gathering information from the locals about the real events leading up to Tavy's death.

Nerves were pulled as tightly as fiddle strings when the siblings broke up into pairs. There was a possibility they were all walking into trouble. Will and Katrina headed to the jail as soon as they passed the outskirts of Adobe Wall.

The small town was known as a trading center. It had a couple of stores, a livery, several saloons, an undertaker, and a cafe. True to its name, all of the buildings were made of adobe, and many were built in a string sharing common walls.

The most remarkable structure was the old, abandoned adobe fort with a dirt floor measuring eighty square feet under a nine feet tall ceiling. It had one entrance which also served as the exit. The Comanche and Kiowa Indians had been hostile and volatile here as late as 1874.

The original settlement had begun as an active buffalo camp and had survived the great Indian battles of 1864 and 1874 within the walls of this fort. After the second battle, the hostilities quieted, and the fort was eventually vacated. The town itself became a notorious hideout for outlaws and thieves.

The jail was a low building like all the other adobes with little ventilation or access to natural light. Will and Kat entered the door, and wood smoke irritated their eyes. The dark interior momentarily put them at a disadvantage until their eyes had time to clear and adjust. The deputy stared at them from a chair with his feet propped on a desk, and they stood there silently staring back.

Will asked the first question.

"Are you the sheriff here?" He tried to get a good look at the man.

"Ah, na, not 'xactly, I'm tha sheriff's deputy. You'd be wantin' to see Jim Hackett, but he's out a tha territory on bidness, law bidness.

"What brings ya here? I reckon yer bidness falls under

my bidness since I'm tha only law 'round."

Will took an instant dislike to the dumpy little man with brown tobacco spittle on his bottom lip and a ragged whiskered chin. He was wearing the badge of a deputy on his shirt.

Kat spoke to him using the directness of her journalistic experiences. Her ease in addressing men as equals was off putting to most.

"We're here looking for information about Tavias Martin Brandt. You recognize the name, don't you? The sheriff in Sweetwater sent us here to ask questions about the telegram he received."

The man's boots dropped to the floor, thudding loudly, and he sat up straighter and stiffer in his chair. His eyes darted from one to the other of the visitors before he spoke. He saw a tall woman dressed like a man and heard her asking nosey questions about a delicate subject.

"Uh, no, I'm not familiar with tha name right off. Why, should I be?" he addressed his answer to the man, not her.

"Wrong answer, Deputy, since he died right here in this very jail. The telegram said he hung himself here. So, yes," Will said, "I think ya should remember 'im."

Kat fired back. "Surely, a lot of accused horse thieves don't take their own lives after you lock 'em up! I'd think the incident would be a hard thing to forget!"

Will added, "He was our brother, and we're here to collect his things and to ask what happened."

The man tilted his head back, looking up at Will, then his chin dropped back into position breaking the eye contact. His expression changed, and he hesitated a minute too long before getting his memory back.

"Òh, yeah, ya don't say? Come ta think of it, ya must be talkin' 'bout tha horse thieving fellow we locked up a while back. Oh, yeah, I 'member now ya mention it. He saved us tha trouble a havin' to hang 'im! Right nice a tha feller too!"

In a loud, annoyed voice, Willheim demanded. "Show us tha holding cell your sheriff locked him in!"

"Now jus' a minute, ya'll can't bust in here and order me aroun' like this is yer town! Ya'll haf ta wait 'til Sheriff Hacket gets back." whined the dirty-faced man.

After a look into his steel-hardened eyes, the man complied.

Will and Kat peered into the tiny, black-iron-barred cubicle with disgust and looked at each other. Then Will reiterated, "My sister asked for his things. Get 'em, an' we'll be on our way."

"I don't know what things ya mean, Mister, 'cause the pris'ner didn't have no things. Somebody musta cleaned 'im out good 'fore tha sheriff brought 'im in here. Not uncommon 'round these parts."

Kat fired back, "One more question--Tavias Brandt was accused of stealing a horse. Whose horse, was it? We aim to speak to this person as well."

"I don't recollect, but the sheriff knows, and I done tol' ya he ain't here."

"Yes, you did."

"Get on out! I gotta ta make my rounds. You've already made me late. Clear on out 'fore I take a notion ta throw ya both in tha same cell I jus' showed ya!"

Once outside, they talked about the beads of perspiration popping out on the deputy's brow. He was definitely covering something up. It looked more and more like Tavy never made it to this jail.

There was still the possibility of an informal lynching the deputy was hiding. The jail cell ceiling was much too low for someone to hang himself.

By this time, Morgan had asked around at a couple of the saloons about Tavy, but no one remembered seeing anyone who fit his description or knew about the incident. No one knew anything about a horse thief from a few weeks back, either.

One bartender thought a horse had been stolen, but it turned out to be as far back as early fall, maybe the first part of September.

Mateas found the undertaker's parlor easily. He was a gray-headed man quite long in the tooth, but his memory was sharp. He kept a meticulous ledger of records. He hadn't buried any strangers in December, but he had sold an empty coffin to the sheriff which wasn't really too unusual.

Except, the undertaker remembered he'd paid for it out of his own pocket. He had thought it odd and had made a specific notation in his ledger in case the sheriff came back later for a receipt to be reimbursed by the county.

There was another thing out of the ordinary too. When the sheriff needed a body buried, he always hired him to do it, but he hadn't asked him this time.

The sheriff hadn't offered any other information, and the undertaker hadn't felt it was his business to ask. The lawman must have had a good reason for the purchase.

Mateas also got information from the drunken hostler at the livery stable. He said the sheriff had hired a wagon late one afternoon to haul a coffin to the cemetery. Mateas was able to pinpoint the day to the same time the empty box had been bought.

The old man had finally remembered the exact day because his brother-in-law had butchered a hog. There was a family supper at his place on the same evening. He'd left the livery to go to the feed shortly after the sheriff picked up the wagon.

Even a drunk would remember something like hog-butchering and a family-gathering to eat the roasted pork. Mateas took his recollection to be accurate. After finding this much out, Mateas rode his horse to the cemetery, east of town. He had no difficulty locating the freshest grave.

Taking off his hat, he knelt at the likely grave of his beloved brother, Tavias. He offered a prayer of

Thanksgiving to the God up above for giving him such a fine brother. Sorrowfully, he read the black lettering on the white, wooden marker.

TAVIAS BRANDT

HORSE THIEF

DECEMBER 1877

Meeting at a predetermined place, the four Brandts compared the information they'd each collected. Will and Kat didn't believe Tavy had ever been in the Adobe Wall jail, and the cell ceiling was too low for a man to hang himself.

Morgan said his body hadn't been taken to the undertaker, but the sheriff had purchased an empty pine coffin in December and paid for it with his own money. He'd found a grave with their brother's name on a wooden marker dated December. It was decided to visit the sign maker.

The man was very affable and forthcoming. He said the sheriff had ordered the white cross grave marker. He remembered it well because he had objected to labeling a man a horse thief without knowing if it was a true statement. A man was always more to God than just what he was thought of by men.

He said Sheriff Hackett was agitated at his reluctance and in a great hurry to get the marker made. He came back a couple of days later to pick it up. The sign maker's wife checked their records to make sure her husband was right. Again, it was recorded the sheriff had paid out of his own pocket without asking for a receipt.

Who was buried in the grave at Adobe Wall? They had to know for sure, so the grim task of digging the coffin up was the next step.

They waited outside of Adobe Wall until the town had bedded down. It was a grizzly task to tackle. Even though it looked doubtful Tavias was buried under the mound of dirt clods in the graveyard.

Chapter 18

One Piece at a Time

Tavias came to with a burning pain in his shoulder. A bullet had been dug out, and the wound was bandaged. The whole length of his arm and the shoulder were stiff. It hurt like a son-of-a-gun!

The memory of the ambush, being trapped, and then getting knocked off of his feet all came back in a rush. Valentine! He had to find a way to get back to her. He prayed Winston had gotten the message off to Will.

Elijah had taken a hit to his leg, and the hot bullet had mercifully gone clear through the meaty part of the thigh without hitting the bone. Obviously, he'd received medical attention too. Tavy couldn't make any sense of why they weren't put down with shots to their heads. It would have been so easy.

Why are we still alive?

It wouldn't be long before he would be very sorry to find out the cruel reason.

Tavy and Elijah had been lowered down into the bottom of a dry cistern. A cover was slid over the opening casting them into darkness. Sporadically, blinding light came from above whenever the covering was pulled back, and a bundle of food scraps was dropped down on top of their heads. A bucket of water was sometimes lowered on a rope.

The stale air in the rock-lined chamber of the cistern reeked of body wastes and the stench of human occupation. After sitting in dark confinement, Tavias became disoriented, but he thought they'd been confined in their own filth for a long time.

Without a warning or reason given, the physical torture of Elijah began, but Tavias was always left untouched. He assumed this stroke of luck was because he wasn't one of the hill people. Tavy likely was of little interest to the regulator's gang because neither of the two clans valued his life. Elijah's people might risk their lives to save him, but family blood was the only blood worth a fight.

Regulator Holt started sending the Saxton clan one fresh piece of Elijah at a time to prove he was still alive. So far, three fingers and an ear had been cut off of his body and delivered to his Pa's door. After each example they meant business was collected, the new wound was agonizingly cauterized with a scorching, hot poker.

Holt, the disgraced former Texas Ranger was a cagey son-of-a-bitch. He didn't dare risk the Saxton hostage dying prematurely of a gangrenous infection. He was the bait after all! Elijah's salty relations would eventually relent and retaliate. The renegades were ready and waiting to massacre the Saxton clan as soon as it was lured out into the open!

Tavy had never seen a man suffer as stoically as his companion. He suffered assault after assault mostly in silence. He didn't cry or complain about the pain and mutilation of his body. It was a blessing he was unconscious most of the time.

Tavy cringed with the scraping sound of the lid being

pushed aside. The noise might mean another ungodly extraction!

Chapter 19

Now What?

~Back at Adobe Wall

Eerily in silence and dread of what they could find had the Brandts standing around Tavy's grave with their heads bowed and holding hands in solidarity. Mateas led the group in a prayer ending in, "Amen," from each person.

Morgan removed the wooden marker and angrily tossed it away. The insult of labeling Tavias a horse thief would never see the light of day again. It would be tossed into the flames of their campfire later.

Pa's two shovels were used to dig. Willheim manned one and Morgan the other. It soon became evident the grave was a shallow one. When the rim of Will's shovel hit something solid with a dull thud, they all moaned.

Four sets of eyes as big as saucers glanced around at each other unsure of what would be found. The tension could have been cut with a butter knife. The sky chose this exact moment to open up, releasing pellets of sharp, stinging sleet. It fell down from heaven encompassing the graveyard as soon as the shovels were employed again to remove the remainder of the dirt.

With the evidence collected thus far in Adobe Wall, Will felt the chance of finding Tavy's body inside had been significantly decreased. There was still room for doubt. Only prying the lid off the mouth of the pine box could reveal the coffin's contents. Time seemed to stop!

Finally, it was Will who held his breath and stooped down to pry the top free.

~Jim Hackett, Sheriff of Adobe Wall

The ashamed and disheartened lawman, Jim Hackett, let his tired horse pick its own pace. It had been a long trip into Indian territory, but he was in no hurry to get back to Adobe Wall. He was feeling guilty about the part he had recently played in the staging of a bold-faced lie. His conscience hurt worse than any physical injury he'd ever suffered.

Blackmail wasn't an excuse, but he had been blackmailed by the man named Jack Holt, a bad man who could ruin Hackett for his past involvement in a crime. Jim thought he had no other choice but to comply or he would be found out. Now, he realized he should have refused and allowed the chips to land where they fell. He was guilty after all.

Dragging his heels back to Adobe Wall with his tail between his legs, the sheriff was oblivious to the discomforts of the winter weather. What he had agreed to do battered his conscience with regret. Covering for Holt's criminal activities to keep himself hidden wasn't worth the anguish.

The Sheriff of Adobe Wall despised himself for not standing up to Holt. He should have refused to be a part of another one of his illegal activities.

Before daybreak, he saw a few lights twinkling through the windows of scattered cabins. He was approaching the outskirts of his town as a more courageous man than the despicable human being who had ridden out. He resolved to make amends for his actions and finally take his punishment.

If I'm not an honest lawman, then I'm no kind of a man at all.

He led his horse to the livery stable and kicked the feet of the hostler sleeping on a pile of hay. The old fool, a worthless drunk, stumbled around to accommodate the sheriff's horse without swapping words.

Hackett walked into the jail to find his useless deputy's feet propped upon the sheriff's desk. He was sound asleep and snoring to beat the band. Hackett walked over and roughly swept his boots off the desk causing them to hit upon the wooden floor. The deputy woke with a start and jumped to his feet ready to fight like a banty rooster. Then he saw it was the sheriff.

"Where have ya been? I was lookin' fer ya ta be back more'n two days ago!" he whined, exposing his yellowed teeth.

The sight of him was sickening, and Jim Hackett knew by his voice something had happened in his absence, and he wasn't going to like it. In no mood to hear bad news, he demanded, "Okay, tell me what's happened."

"They was here, Sheriff, a couple of 'em, a tall pushy female 'n' a hard-jawed man--askin' questions 'n' a wantin' his things!" The deputy rushed his words, and they ran together.

"Slow down, ya darn fool! Tell me exactly what happened. Who was here? You're makin' no sense a'tall. Start from the beginning!"

Marking his place, the sheriff reclaimed the chair and sat behind his desk. If anyone was going to sit here and put his feet up, it would damn sure be him as long as he was still a sheriff!

Simpson was out of breath as he continued sniveling.

"The man, the man we never had, the one who didn't hang 'imself, but ya tol' me to say he did! I hepped ya to bury 'im, jus' did like ya said!

"They's all over me askin' questions, demandin' his things 'n' all tha like. I didn' know what ta say! Ya never tol' me what ta say! Why didn' ya tell me his kin might show up?"

The sheriff caught the drift and sat up straight in his chair. "Aw, hell 'n' damnation!

"Shut up, you stupid fool! When was this? Calm the hell down! What else did they want to know? Tell me exactly."

After the deputy spilled the beans, Jim Hackett went immediately to the grave in the cemetery. Sure enough, it had been dug up and laid open. The lid on the empty pine box was cock-eyed, and footprints were all over. The cross he'd put on the grave was completely gone.

They likely figured Tavy Brandt, or whoever he really was, hadn't been in Adobe Wall at all, and they had figured it right. Discovering this gave them a most important piece to their puzzle. How long would it be before they found out about Holt? My Lord, they could already be on the way to Albuquerque, Texas.

He'd best get word to him. He should know Tavias Brandt's family was nosing around and looking for him. Then, he was washing his hands of this illegal mess he had been forced to fake.

I'll remove and clean up any traces of this empty grave before the night is over.

Chapter 20

Albuquerque, Texas

Willheim took off at a fast clip toward the San Antone territory with his sister right beside him. Morgan sent them off on the road as soon as they discovered the empty shell of a coffin. He and Mateas would catch up with them later.

They'd found not one trace of legitimate evidence Tavy had ever been in Adobe Wall. Why was such an elaborate ruse staged? A hell of a lot of effort went into covering something up for what reason? It was more important than ever to get to the bottom of this mystery. Where was their brother?

The strange message from Tavy was the only lead left to follow. He and Kat were on the way to check out the Post Office in Albuquerque, Texas first. It had been posted there. He feared time might be running out to find Tavy safe. Willheim wouldn't stop looking until he did.

He prayed Tavy was still alive. A sense of urgency drove him southeast as fast as possible. He and Kat pushed Rope Tail and Buckeye hard. The horses were strong and able to keep up with the pace. The riders stopped only to rest them. While the animals grazed unburdened by saddles, supplies, and gear Will and Katrina cat napped.

Brother and sister traveled day and night eating beef jerky and rich pemmican in the saddle. Pemmican was a Native American mixture of tallow, bits of dried meat, and berries guaranteed to keep strength up. It provided an energy boost. Will and Kat were hell bent on a course to reach the Gonzales County line.

Maybe at the Albuquerque Post Office they'd get the next clue to follow by asking the right questions. Who had addressed this envelope? Where could they find the person who mailed it?

Will was grateful Kat was riding beside him. Tavy, Will, and Katrina had ridden together often growing up. Her stamina to keep going combined with her resilience in the cold were an asset. She had not faltered once in the nasty winter conditions with little rest or food. He knew men who weren't as tough as Katrina Brandt.

Both of them were loaded for bear and much better armed than people would notice. Pa had always said, "Clean your guns in public, only if you're looking to have them taken away. Always have something up your sleeve and handy."

They both followed his wise advice always. Gun belts and rifles were visible, but the total of all their weapons was not. The reality of staying alive against an opponent could come down to taking the threat by surprise.

Eveready for the possibility of trouble ahead, Will and Kat double-checked their firearms, making sure they were loaded and in place. They assessed ammunition supplies for reloading. Each pocketed two extra loaded cylinders quickly available to exchange for spent ones.

They rode into the town of Albuquerque one afternoon. A few whitewashed buildings had windowpanes, and storefronts with cleanly swept boardwalks in front. Finding the livery with hay and grain for their weary horses was the first stop for them. The horses had earned and needed attention and time to rest.

They spotted a café for a hot meal later, but their next stop had to be the Post Office. It was getting late in the day. They had to get information from someone before the doors closed for the day.

They entered the small building full of hope and were welcomed by the heat of a woodstove. A handsome, gray-headed woman was sorting papers behind a counter. A Postmaster was likely to know most everyone in the county. Sooner or later, every resident probably made it into the Post Office to pick up or to post mail.

The woman stared at the man accompanied by an uncommonly dressed woman in britches and a leather coat. She was wearing a Stetson. Both people were armed with guns in heavy belts, and each had a hunting knife handy. The man came to the counter holding out an envelope clutched in his hand.

The cowboy touched his hat and introduced the two as Willheim and Kat Brandt.

"Ma'am, could you tell me if you've ever seen this envelope?"

She reached out her hand. "Hand it to me. If it came through here, I'll know it."

Once in her hand, she adjusted the spectacles on her nose before saying, "By the way, my name is Hattie. Glad to meet you."

She studied the envelope for just a moment, then laughed out loud.

"One of the boys from up in the hills brought this to me. He was quite secretive about it but never offered to say why. The envelope was already dirty by the time I got hold of it. The people from those hills aren't known for cleanliness, especially the men. Most can't read or write a lick, either.

"Missionaries came through these parts some time

back and tried to teach the women and girls for a short while. Some learned their letters and numbers, but not much else. The feuding got so bad up there, the missionaries grew afraid and slipped away in the night.

"Winston Saxton brought this letter to me. He has a mama, a couple of sisters, I reckon, and a whole passel of ornery brothers. It's my guess the older sister penciled this scribble across the envelope. He had the coins it took to send it off to Sweetwater. Winston is a special boy, if you get my drift."

"How so Ma'am?"

"I'll try to explain. He's gentle, thoughtful, and kinder than most of his people. Winston isn't sharp but neither is he dangerous. Most of the men living up there are rougher and meaner. Winston is shaded in the head though, a real slow thinker if you know what I mean.

"He's harmless enough and comes to Albuquerque occasionally but always alone. He likes to visit the Post Office because I'll take the time to talk with him. I like him."

"So, his name is Winston? We're looking for our brother. We think whoever posted this will know where he is."

Hattie pointed a finger at him and said, "His whole name is Winston Saxton.

"You know, I thought you looked kind of familiar when you first walked in the door, but I couldn't put my finger on where I'd seen you before. Now, I see it wasn't you at all, though! Lordy, it must have been your brother I saw! Well, I declare! Oh, how, you two do favor!

"Winston lives in those high hills. No outsider with any sense goes up there. It's a wild, wild place with different laws than down here where reasonable people live."

"He's here in town, then, our brother?" Kat asked excitedly.

"I doubt it. I only saw the man one time, and it must have been weeks ago."

Will said, "So, tell us where we can find this hill boy, Winston Saxton."

"Well, you won't find him unless he wants to find you. In the hills, they all slink around like animals. They know every nook and cranny of the rough country, and they melt into the trees when strangers show up. They're always feuding, fighting, and pulling off ugly tricks among themselves. It doesn't stop there, either. Sometimes they kill each other.

"If you're determined, I suppose if you go south and keep following Sandies Creek you might run across somebody who might know something. Be careful and keep your eyes and ears open all the time," Hattie advised.

This woman had been a wealth of information. The fact she had seen Tavy was a relief. It gave their spirits a boost.

It was late afternoon when they walked out of the Post Office. Hattie put a closed sign on the door as they left, and they heard the lock click behind them. From there, they walked over to the café they'd spotted earlier. The special supper was a beefsteak dinner with custard pie and coffee.

They ate without talking, with the intent on gobbling down the hot food like field hands. They were exhausted, filthy, and hadn't been warm on both sides at once in days. At the hotel, they rented two rooms and enough hot water for baths.

Early the next morning a few people were milling on the street and beginning to enter and exit doors. Willheim and Kat ate a big breakfast of eggs, biscuits, sausage gravy, and coffee at the café. Afterwards, they collected their refreshed horses and headed south out of town.

They went in the direction Hattie had directed them yesterday. The father away they got, it turned into tangled, rough country quickly. Both horses were game to go where pointed.

Tavias must be close, and they wouldn't stop until they found him.

Chapter 21

Jack Helt, the Regulator

Jack Holt read the telegram from Jim Hackett, the sheriff at Adobe Wall, and wadded it up. One of his men had returned with the paper when he came back with supplies from Albuquerque. Holt roared and stomped around the camp in an irrational fit of temper for over an hour or more.

Jim Hackett blew it! He let him down, and Holt would make the coward pay dearly. Right now, he had to get on the stick and push the hill people harder until they reacted to the kidnapping of Elijah Saxton and the torture he was enduring. He had to force his clan to attack the camp, so his men could obliterate as many of them as possible.

Jack was blindsided to learn Tavy Brandt, an outsider who had gotten himself caught up in this war, had so many earnest family members willing to hunt for him in the dead of winter. With luck any search would have ended at Adobe Wall, but Holt had never been a man with the winds of luck at his back.

He had to accelerate his plan considerably to draw the hill people out into the open so he could put them down and then get himself the hell out of this territory. No doubt, reputable Texas Rangers, representing Texas law, were coming after him!

Jack Holt was a disgraced ranger who had been demoted to the dregs of a regulator hired only to clean up messes. He was a man who disrespected the law and stepped over the into the realm of being an outlaw himself. His lack of empathy fueled an insatiable lust for killing.

Dammit to hell, the Texas Rangers might already be in Gonzales County closing in on him!

A tight spot was percolating around him. Holt intended to give the hornet's nest the hardest shake yet. This time he needed to extract a bigger piece of Elijah Saxton's flesh to draw the clansmen out. He'd deliver the entirety of a foot amputated above Elijah's ankle to Pa Saxton!

Surely, the horror of it would rile him enough to take action! Thus far, he'd only sent small pieces of the boy and had not stirred a response. A whole foot would be a significant, bloody mess. It just might tip the scales and cause the showdown he desired! This had been a lot of fun, but Holt was feeling heat breathing down his neck.

The clock was ticking!

Chapter 22

Where Is Tavias?

Will had no idea where the icy Sandie Creek was leading them. He was tense and alert for anything, noise or movement. His obedient brush dogs were hanging close. Buckeye's and Rope Tail's nostrils flared, and their heads occasionally bobbed in nervous movements.

Will and Kat kept tension on their reins to better navigate the tight, unfamiliar terrain. The brush and undergrowth grew thick here, and the path narrowed forcing them to move in single file. Will led the dogs with his sister bringing up the rear.

The cowboy signed to his dogs to keep quiet and not break rank. Katrina drew his attention when she audibly gasped. He glanced back to see her head tipped back and followed her line of vision, but he only caught a glimpse of movement. He only saw enough to imagine it could have been an animal, a bird or something else displaced by the wind.

"What'd ya see, Kat?" he whispered, hoarsely.

"Don't know. Whatever it was moved too quickly to

be sure," his sister whispered.

"It was in my peripheral vision for only a moment, then gone. It was definitely something. For a moment I even thought it might be a person."

The dogs had caught the scent of something and were raring to be released, but Will still held them back. He gave Rope Tail enough head to pick the pace though. Buckeye followed right on the heels of the dogs. Could the journey to find Tavy be taking a turn?

Willheim sent Indigo alone to scout ahead. As soon as his frantic, stationary barking commenced in earnest, he released Red Dog and Blacksmith to join him. Soon, it was evident by the ruckus the dogs definitely had something cornered. The frantic fracas led the riders to a compact clearing where Indigo, Blacksmith and Red Dog had a small figure treed like a raccoon.

All three were growling and snarling at the base of a large oak marking the bark with their claws. They were desperate to scrabble higher. The fearsome racket unsettled the horses trapped in such a tight space.

A grimy, ragged boy used his legs to hold on for dear life in the branches of a tree. The stance he took freed his hands to let fly a stone from a slingshot. The rock hit Red Dog in the head causing him to let out a sudden cry of pain and drop back.

He next took aim at Willheim. The moment the boy's eyes landed on his face. They opened wider. His movements stalled, and Will was mighty glad when he lowered the slingshot.

Taking advantage of the reprieve, Will spoke over the din loudly but calmly enough to take control of the situation with a calm voice of reason. He assumed this was the boy Hattie mentioned. He took a gamble and used the name he'd picked up.

"I'll call my dogs off, Winston, if you give yer word not ta fire tha slingshot again. We're friendly. We've come a long way looking fer ya. Hattie sent us. We don't mean ya any harm, just want to talk to ya is all. We're lookin' for Tavy. Do ya know where he is?"

The solemn-faced boy continued to stare directly at Willheim's face, but at least he did lower the weapon. The man blew a short, sharp whistle, and the dogs silenced, stepped back, and sat on their haunches, waiting. Rope Tail relaxed immediately causing Buckeye to calm down.

Neither Will nor Kat made a move, and the boy stayed solidly wedged in the tree, waiting.

Kat called up. "At the Post Office, Hattie told us about you, Winston. She told us to find the good boy named Winston who lived in these hills."

He nodded once. His speech faltered, but he finally said, "Name's Winston. Hattie's my frien'."

"Yeah, Hattie likes you too, Winston. We're looking for our brother, Tavias. Have you seen him?"

"We need to get to him."

Again, he bobbed his head looking in Will's direction.

"Ya sure do look most like 'im, Mister, he figgered yu'd be cumin ta hep, sure did hope ya wud. I give Ms. Hattie his messige like he tol' me. Gave her tha money for postin' like he sed. I did it all jest liken I'se 'sposed to."

"Ya did really good, Winston, really, really good." Grinning with encouragement, Will bragged on the boy. "I'll tell 'im ya did it 'xactly like he told ya. He must trust ya a lot, Son."

Winston reached into his pocket and pulled out a shiny gold watch and chain.

"Tavy give me this here timepiece, ere ya fixin' to take it back, Mister?"

Kat gently answered to assure him. "No, no we won't take it away, Winston. It's a gift to you from Tavy. He likes his watch 'n' must want you to have it."

Looking back at Will, Winston said, "Mister, ya look awful like 'im, I thought ya wuz 'im at fust."

"I know I look like him, Son. I'm 'is brother, Will. This lady is his sister, Kat. Can ya take us ta Tavy?"

"Nah, don't reckon, he might be ded by now, maybe, he's with my brother, 'lija. Lija's hurt somethin' awful baid, they's cutting 'im up in peecis."

Will's muscles stiffened. "Can ya take us to your pa then or someone else maybe. We're not leaving 'til we see somebody who knows what's happened."

"Pa'll be madder than a wet hen iffen I do, he don' trus' no strangers 'roun. Tavy saved my life, I reckin ya kin foller me 'n' see what Pa sez. I can't promise ya nothin'."

It wasn't long until they were lost or so it seemed to Will. He was turned around and had trouble keeping his sense of direction in this dense growth and following game trails. It took a whole lot to spook him, but the hair was standing up on the dogs' necks, and their low growls made his skin crawl.

He smelled wood smoke and looked up to a hazy, ribbon of it rising before the source came into view. The dogs were getting more and more antsy, and he ordered them to settle down.

Out of nowhere, four men stepped out from between the trees surrounding them. The business ends of their scatter guns were aimed at Will's and Kat's chests. The tattered men were definitely capable of shooting!

Just as Winston had warned, they weren't welcomed.

"Who be ye?" the one in front of them yelled.

Winston spoke up. "These be Tavy's kin. He sed they'd be comin!"

One of the four guards silently melted back into the trees and disappeared. Soon, an older man showed up and penetrated the strangers and the dogs with beady eyes. He too held a squirrel gun directed at them.

"I kin see ya favor 'im, aright."

"Git off yer horses, 'n' foller Winston ezy like ta tha house up yonder. I'm thinkin' we best be swapin' sum words."

The culture in these back lumpy hills of South Texas was clearly simple and primitive. Winston's people were unfriendly and suspicious of flatlanders. It was obvious these men were dangerous and unpredictable. Even inside Pa Saxton's home the atmosphere was tense.

Will and Kat were tersely herded by two of the captors into a large one-room log cabin. Two of the armed men stayed on the large porch with Winston and his pa.

A rough-hewn table sat in the middle of the room with benches on either side for seating. At each end a handmade, straight-backed chair with tightly woven rope seats sat. Will and Kat were unceremoniously motioned to sit down.

There was a rough ladder leading up to a full upper loft. There was a bed pushed against a wall on one side of the cabin. One corner of the room was partitioned off by a woven spread hanging across a wire. The home was tidy enough, and the floor had been swept clean.

A fire was popping in the big fireplace, and the cook stove was hot. It was the first time they'd had a chance to rest and get warm since they left Albuquerque. The heat was a relief from the winter chill.

So far, Will had counted seven offspring, six boys, counting Winston and the missing Elija, and one almost grown girl he was seeing for the first time. She was pretty with a good figure, full lips, and long, yellow hair, but her eyes were strangely hollow like those of a frightened, beaten dog. She held her head mostly down and never looked directly at the visitors.

She worked silently beside her ma in the corner dedicated to the cooking. There was a big pot steaming, and the aroma of boiling meat permeated the air. The smell of bread was coming from the oven.

The door they'd entered suddenly pushed open, scraping across the threshold. Mr. Saxton entered, and his posture and movements were those of a weary man. He removed his hat and threw it to the side without even looking, and it landed neatly onto a hook sticking out of the wall. He took his seat in one of the chairs.

The two women came directly with mugs of strong, dark, bitter, hot chicory coffee along with coarsely ground cornmeal dodgers, wild onions, and pickles. A crockery of butter and another of thick, blackstrap molasses was set out to slather on the fried cornbread.

After they broke bread, Mr. Saxton commenced to explain the complicated situation from the beginning.

The citizens of Albuquerque had grown leery of the feuding in the hills. They didn't like it and felt threatened. The town leaders contacted Austin and requested the Texas Rangers be sent for their protection. The outside friction started right after.

Since the rangers had nearly disbanded after the Indian wars, many of the lawmen returned to their families. The ranger force had been left shorthanded. There had even been talk of disbanding the Texas Rangers altogether.

The capital of Austin couldn't spare rangers and sent the regulator, Jack Holt, instead. He used to be a Texas Ranger but now only led a few ruthless men willing to fight. Texas officials unwittingly unleashed bullying out for blood on the hill people.

The situation in the high country was tense and growing more so by the day. Two opposed family clans had feuded off and on for years, mostly aggravating each other. When the regulator had shown up claiming to be an arm of the law sent to clean the families out, things had gotten violent.

The two families joined together in a temporary truce to help each other run this regulator and his men off of the hills. The clansmen formed a unified alliance. The conflict had turned out to be harder and longer than they had thought.

Finally, Mr. Saxton started telling what he knew of

Tavy's and Elijah's kidnapping. Following the account, he said Winston had found where Holt and his gang were holding them

The vicious devil started sending small bloody pieces of his son, Elijah, to his doorstep proving he was still alive.

Saxton couldn't rightly say if Tavy was still alive or not, but the last Winston had seen of them, they were together.

Winston burst through the door breathlessly, excited, and talking fast!

"Pa, they's a rider cumin up tha backside a tha ridge, a cumin fast 'n' totin 'nother bloody sack 'n' it's a bigger, bloodier un this time!"

Will's dogs along with Saxton's penned hounds set to barking and baying. Before the Saxtons could react and uncover the defense hatches in the walls, a dull, heavy sound thumped against the back door making it jolt and rattle.

Ma Saxton let out the pitiful cry of a grieved mother. It filled the cabin with a dark, ominous sound of doom. The girl noiselessly disappeared behind the spread strung across the corner of the room.

The rider never slowed down, and he disappeared faster than he'd ridden into the yard. When the commotion subsided, one of the Saxton men opened the door just enough to drag a bloody sack inside. Blood smeared a stripe on the wooden floor.

Will was certain Kat had seen more things on the trail than any woman should, but her hands were clamped together over her mouth in horror, and her eyes were big and round.

He was just as affected when an unwelcome flashback of the soiled toweling wrapped around Adam's severed hand took over. The memory of the stench of rotting flesh as he carried it off to bury filled his nostrils again.

He struggled to hold back the burning bile crawling up

his throat as Elijah's foot, cut off above the ankle, was unwrapped and identified. Will immediately recognized it didn't have the characteristics of his brother's foot.

He was relieved, but the Saxtons identified Elijah's big toe and pinky toe. A dreadful somber mood was cast over the whole family.

Will had listened to the sorted tale of the feuding families, the Saxtons and the Butlers. He'd heard about the renegade Texas Regulator who was as ruthless as a rabid dog. Any hint of calm and clear thinking escaped him after seeing the human foot lying on the floor.

His thoughts ran wild with the possible conditions and dangers Tavias might be experiencing at this very moment. Even the possibility he was already dead seemed preferable to slow, deliberate mutilation. He and his sister must go immediately to rescue their brother, but where would they start? They didn't know or understand this hill country or its culture!

Mr. Saxton advised Tavy's kin to stay put and out of sight in the cabin until Winston returned with Mr. Butler, the leader of the Butler clan. Winston had already run off to fetch Terrance Butler.

What was less than two hours seemed like a full day of waiting. The cabin was quiet with the Saxtons and the Brandts cleaning and checking all their weapons and stores of ammunition more than once. Mrs. Saxton served a thickened meat stew and biscuits with honey. The yellow-haired girl sat alone in her corner piecing quilt blocks and never looking up from her work. Her cheeks were shiny with tears, and she kept wiping at the moisture.

Suddenly, the door opened, and all guns simultaneously pointed toward the breach. A giant of a man with shaggy, white hair and a long beard stepped inside the room led by Winston. It was Butler, head of his clan. Guns were lowered. The table cleared except for Saxton, Butler, and the Brandts.

Willheim listened and asked astute questions. Butler drew a map for him on a piece of brown, wrinkled paper. He marked where Elijah and Tavy were being held in relationship to where they were sitting at the table.

The heads of both clans agreed the showdown was past due. The price could be high before it was over. Many could die on both sides after the first shot was fired, but the regulator had to be decimated.

In a moment of stolen privacy, Willheim took his baby sister outside supposedly to check on their horses and dogs. Once in the barn he wrapped her in his brotherly arms and hugged her close, kissing her cheek.

"You best sit this one out, Katrina. Leave it to me to fight for the both of us."

"Not a chance, Brother! I won't be left behind! I'll do my own riding and my own fighting for Tavias, for our family! My convictions are as strong as yours, Willheim. Besides, you and I both know I'm the better shot," she smiled, punching him hard in the arm.

He feigned pain. "Yeah, I don't doubt it, Katrina, but this will be a vicious fight, and we'll be caught right in the middle of it. If you're determined to do this, Sis, keep your tail covered and your head down. Skedaddle if things go to shit."

"Listen to me, Will! Same goes for you."

The danger was understood between them as they strapped heavy gun belts in place and saddled Brush Tail and Buckeye. Soon, the Saxtons, Butlers, and Brandts would be ready to ride out.

The weather had taken a nasty turn. A bitter cold north wind blew bringing with it freezing mist. There was no way to know how close Morgan and Mateas might be. It was a worry the two might ride into the fight.

Chapter 23

The Bona Fide Texas Rangers

The first stop in town for Morgan and Mateas was the Post Office to ask if Will and Kat had been there. The Postmaster remembered them well. They'd ridden up into the hills a couple of days ago looking for Tavias and a boy. She suggested they talk to the Texas Rangers who'd ridden in from Austin today before going into the hill country in the morning.

It was a divine, intervention their journey and the rangers' journey had intersected. The parallels of their purposes would create an alliance. Just happening to run into the Texas Rangers at this juncture was fortuitous.

There was only one café so locating the rangers ready to eat supper was easy enough. Morgan asked if he and Mateas could join them, and tables were readily pushed together. After Morgan explained they needed to go south into the hill country in the morning, the captain readily offered for the two men to go along with them at dawn.

The captain and his men were sent here because of a telegram received by the Texas Rangers' Office in Austin from Sheriff Jim Hackett at Adobe Wall. The sheriff confessed his part in covering up a crime for the regulator, Jack Holt. Holt had blackmailed him into cooperating in a crime.

It outlined the sheriff's specific lies and actions perpetrated to keep the whereabouts of an innocent man a secret. Jim Hackett had staged a crime, death, and burial of a man named Tavias Brandt. Then he tendered his resignation and turned himself into the Austin authorities.

Morgan told the in-depth story bringing Mateas, Willheim, and Katrina, and him to South Texas in the dead of winter. The two separate stories fleshed together as one.

The rangers had been sent to drag Holt, the regulator, and his outlaws back to Austin to face justice. Morgan and Mateas were here to find Willheim and Kat who came here ahead of them from Adobe Wall. The Brandts were here collectively to find their missing brother. All of them were set to crash into one bullseye on the same target.

They were headed right into the mouth of a perfect storm. This was all in the hands of God.

Chapter 24

A Journalist's Perspective

~Katrina Brandt

Katrina had a knack for writing. She fed this talent by noticing even the smallest details of what was going on around her. She absorbed events by observing, listening, smelling, tasting, and feeling emotions. Her personalized style brought her perspectives to life on a written page.

Newspaper editors back east were hungry for her submissions. The readers saw the west and its characters through her eyes. She had the ability to paint vivid pictures with words.

As clansmen assembled outside of Pa Saxton's house preparing to fight, Kat was fascinated by this subculture frozen in time. People at the base of the hills and beyond were changing all the while these in the hills were not. Above and below the line, the two cultures were worlds apart.

Isolation and lack of education shaped this splintered cluster of human beings. They appeared, spoke, and lived only with what had been passed down to them.

Vocabulary was salted with butchered English words missing letters, beginnings, and endings. Pronunciations were in a thick dialect. Colorful phrases, sayings, inferences, and meanings made communication difficult and misunderstood by outsiders.

Clothing was passed down through the family until it was good for nothing but rags. They wore faded sewn over patches. Nothing was wasted here.

Old, handmade family possessions were still being used. Newer, handcrafted items made by younger generations were still primitive but impressive works of art. The items reflected basic techniques and designs from the past but with a flourish of creativity.

Weapons were carried by men and boys of all ages. Many were outdated, but they could use them with accuracy. Transportation depended on mules, donkeys, and brushtail mustangs. Two-wheeled carts were very popular, but many traveled on foot.

Music was played in intriguing rhythms on old, improvised, and handmade instruments. Corn liquor was cooked. It was sold, traded, bartered, and quite plentiful. The land and wildlife were respected for sustaining sustenance and providing income.

Men started arriving on Pa Saxton's land as soon as word of the pending fight circulated through the Saxton and Butler clans. Kat wisely tied and tucked her long, brown hair beneath her Stetson. Her uncommon height for a woman helped keep her gender from being an issue. The weapons she toted plus the big stallion helped too. Her britches, leathers, and the natural cowhide coat were all things men wore.

Jugs of moonshine were passed around as the men talked, whittled, and waited. She took a swig and forced herself not to gasp and cough. It had a kick!

When it came time to move out, the group rode away

from the Saxton cabin under an icy mist with a frigid wind whistling through the trees. The stormy winter weather was both a trial and a blessing. It muted their movements and increased the chances of moving out unnoticed.

The goals were to extract Elijah and hopefully Tavias from the devils who held them. In the process, the Holt gang would be wiped out. At least it was the plan.

She wondered about Morgan and Mateas. Where might they be? Both were excellent trackers. They'd find a way to join them. She didn't dare predict more because the reality of this raid could backfire.

She reached forward and rubbed Buckeye's neck speaking to him with affection. She reined him closer alongside Rope Tail. At the adjustment, Will turned his head in her direction and winked encouragement, but his usual, easy-going smile didn't follow the familiar gesture.

The brush dogs followed on his horse's heels like three good soldiers. Their coats stood up, insulating them from the cold and making them look more menacing. The muscles of Willheim's jaw worked rhythmically. The big brother and little sister exchanged solemn glances. No words were needed between them as anything needing to be said had been said.

Noise from the enemy's camp was heard before the source of the commotion was seen. The hill people were accustomed to skirmishes and silently spread-out blindly encircling the outside edge of the target. The darkness and falling sleet hampered visibility considerably.

When the signal of the owl's hoot sounded, the mass started in unison to cautiously move closer. They were in place to heed the next signal to swarm in and scatter like ants at a picnic.

With guns drawn and reins held between her teeth, Kat used her strong legs squeezing Buckeye forward and then leg reining him to surge leftward in advancement. The clansmen, with a great tumult of unearthly hollering and swearing, charged in a devastating rush, catching the enemies' camp off guard.

Holt's men were caught off guard drinking, carousing, and also making a loud den of chaotic revelry until realizing they had been infiltrated. Almost at the same moment a sizeable kerosene-fed bonfire exploded into angry, licking tongues. The flames lit up the theater allowing everyone to see better. The timing couldn't have been planned at such a perfect time.

Kat was horrified when the reason for the scene playing out became clear. She realized the bastards were assembled in the storm for a lynching party. At the time, she didn't fathom the regulator had ordered Elijah and Tavy to be hung by their necks. Their bodies and other evidence were to be thrown onto the raging flames of the bonfire.

Neither could she have had any idea her brothers along with the Texas Rangers were close by. They were coming for Holt and his gang of misfits.

Outlaws wouldn't miss a boot-jerking hanging, not even to avoid standing in the sleet. They lived for the thrills of such violence. The entire camp waited outside their shelters for the gruesome event to begin.

Sleet started coming down harder and still the criminals stood their ground. They were drunk and not one had a horse saddled or handy except for two horses waiting under the biggest tree.

Kat barely registered the sound of new guns from the north. She spared a lightning quick glance and caught only a glimpse of Mateas exiting from the thicket. His dark, shiny skin color was wet and highlighted by light from the fire.

This is when she spotted her sweet Tavias, thin and beaten with hands tied behind his back and a noose around his neck. He sat perched precariously on one of two horses. On the second horse sat a man, Elijah probably, slumped completely over. Every muscle in her body responded to the flood of adrenaline pumping through her veins. She braced for what had to be done.

Fearing the two animals could bolt spurred by all the racket and confusion around them, she poised to kick Buckeye into a run. If those horses took off, the jerk of the drop would leave the men in the air to swing and the ropes to snap their necks.

Before Katrina could take flight to save Tavy, one of Holt's men, desperate to steal her horse and get away, pulled her hard to the ground. He grabbed Buckeye's long mane and made a giant leap. He scrambled to get seated in the saddle. His clumsiness offered Kat a small window in which to act.

She whistled shrilly and Buckeye automatically reacted by rearing on his hind legs and landing on his forelegs. He reared and bucked head to tail in the air like a wild bronco. It only took Buckeye two bucks to throw the scum summersaulting high into the air. He fell hard on the ground several feet away.

Kat shot and nailed the man twice in the gut. In only a few seconds, she was back in Buckeye's saddle. A blood-curdling, three-syllable scream yodeled from her throat. It was an Indian war cry to count coup for killing an opponent. She'd never had a reason to use it before, but she was glad to now.

~Will

In the meantime, try as he might, Willheim couldn't reach Tavy before a man trying to flee the massacre pulled the horse right out from under his brother. Will's bullet hit he man in the forehead, and the horse ran away with the dead man still on it!

Will got to Tavy and supported his light weight. He stood on Rope Tail's saddle, cutting the rope from Tavy's neck with his hunting knife. He laid his emaciated brother like a baby onto the icy ground. His head was tilted at an unnatural angle, but he was alive.

Will knelt over Tavy who was laboring for every breath of the frosty air. He removed his heavy coat and covered him from the storm.

Tavy had stared straight at Will, meeting his eyes just before the horse jolted out from under him. Tavias knew Willheim had come for him. Tavias was struggling hard to say something.

"Don't try ta talk, Tavy! I'm gonna get ya out a here 'n' to a doctor! There'll be plenty a time for us ta talk later. Save yer strength!"

"Nahh, pra-pramis … me-Val-a-tin…I knew yuued com to saf 'er…my Val-en-tin, Wil…"

Will stroked his brother's face and head endearingly.

"Don't talk, Tavy, course I'm here, came as fast as I could find ya, we're all here, Morgan, me, Mateas, and little Kat, not sa little anymore! Pa sent us ta get ya, he wants ya home."

"Promis… get Valen, pramis." Tavy's eyes were fixed in place on Will's face just before his life left him. They glazed over, and a loud, rattling breath expelled from his mouth.

Will shouted, so afraid and yet knowing Tavy couldn't hear him anymore.

"I will, I will, I will, I swear it, I will! Where is it? Where do I look?"

But it was too late for an answer. Tavy had given up the Holy Ghost and passed into heaven where nothing could ever hurt him again. The pellets of sleet bounced off his still, gaunt whiskered face. Perfectly shaped balls fell through the spaces in the mass of his tangled hair.

Willheim could hear Katrina weeping at his shoulder. He saw two sets of boots and legs standing on the other side. He knew without looking Morgan and Mateas were there.

The Brandt family had lost a true treasure in this cold, miserable winter storm. Will didn't even notice the whole area had grown quieter.

Chapter 25

Tavy's Valentine

Tracking down Tavy's valentine led directly back to Pa Saxton's door. Turned out, Valentine was a real, live person and not a thing he could just fold up and tuck in his pocket. He approached Mr. Saxton with hat in hand, turning it round and round nervously.

"Sir, I've heard ya have a daughter here by tha name a Valentine. I think maybe I saw her when I was here before."

"Yeah, that'd be bout right." He paused to spit a brown stream of bacci juice from his lips. "Tavy, now, he'd a spoke fer 'er, but now he's a gone, I reckon tha's tha end of it."

"Well, no, Mr. Saxton, it's not the end 'cause you and my brother shook hands on it after givin' ya financial compensation. You gave yer word on top of it, 'n' the way I see it, this is a done deal. A deal's a deal.

"Me 'n' my brothers 'n' sister, doubled back to yer door ta gather up his intended. Tavy had a powerful love fer yer Valentine. He made me promise with his dyin'

138

breath ta take 'er back to Sweetwater with me.

"I vowed to 'im I'd fetch her."

Winston had told Willhelm how the deal had been made between Tavy and his Pa. Will didn't have faith in Mr. Saxton's honor, so he'd tried to push the man into a corner. Saxton's family had just buried their eldest son, Elijah, this morning and were already tipsy on moonshine.

Will doubted he'd want trouble like having to return Tavy's money when he didn't likely still have it.

"Looky here, what ya promised yer ded brother ain't no bidness a mine. Here abouts we take cere a our own 'n' we keep what's ours. They twern't married er nothin', so ya ain't no claim ta say nothin' 'bout what happins ta 'er.

"Ya sed yer piece 'n' I sed mine. We ain't got nothin else ta be jawin' 'bout," the man said emphatically.

He had no idea how equally determined Willheim Brandt was to keep his word to Tavias.

"Is there no way you'd consider lettin' her go live with Tavy's family, at least fer a while?"

Saxton gripped his chin with a dirty hand thinking on the matter. After a spell, he looked Will over with his bloodshot eyes.

"Tha onliest way yu'll be takin my girl outta this here cabin is ta marry 'er proper yersef 'n' throw in a poke a dollers a yer own."

"Sir, I aim to do it, then, state yer terms," Will answered.

"Ya ain't even jawed with tha girl, tarnation, yer a pecular, cus. Er ya right shore? If ya er, I want Tav's hose 'n', riggin ta stay in my barn, 'n' fifty dollars, 'n' his new carbine he lef' here."

Will looked the man straight back into his eyeballs and held out his hand to seal the deal.

"Done, then! I guess it's 'bout time I meet tha girl who's 'bout ta be my wife."

His siblings mumbled cautions and uncertainties as

they followed Will and the old man into the cabin. Shockingly, he'd just sold his daughter a second time for money without even consulting her.

Willheim's eyes roamed around the cabin searching for the female he figured to be Valentine. When Will and Kat had been here before he'd had tunnel vision set only on locating Tavy. He barely remembered the pretty yellow-haired girl with sad eyes.

Now, in the kitchen corner, there were three females. One he knew to be Ma Saxton, and the other two in pigtails looked like kids. Will thought them to be about ten years old. He surely hoped neither was considered of marrying age.

Mr. Saxton bellowed, abruptly, "Valen, git yersef out here! Tavy's kins a come to clect ya!"

From the corner of the room where the spread was strung for privacy, a puffy-eyed young girl with long, yellow hair and a slight frame bashfully emerged.

It was indeed the girl he'd seen before. She was cleaner and less scruffy than the other Saxtons then and now. Will thought if her face wasn't so forlorn she'd be not just pretty but beautiful. The evidence of sorrow threatened to break Will's already broken heart.

Her eyes were downcast toward the cracked and worn-out leather of her oversized boots. She rolled her eyes up stealing a quick, unsure glance of this man who looked so like Tavias.

Will knew the close resemblance he shared with Tavy.

He cleared his throat, aware everyone in the room was watching and listening.

"Miss Valentine, Ma'am, my brother loved you. His last words were about your future. He cared more for you than he cared for himself. I promised him I'd take you back to Sweetwater with me to live with his people. Your pa says you can't go with me unless you agree to marry me.

"I want to marry you today in my brother's place,

Valentine, if you'll do me the honor."

Valentine looked up at her pa briefly and then back at the floor, waiting. The decision was his to make, not hers.

Pa Saxton spoke.

"It's fittin' Tavy's brother takes 'is place. It's tha way a tha hills, right enuff. Tha prechter'll be fetched soon as I kin get words to 'im."

Willheim refused to show the disgust he felt for her pa. He looked compassionately toward her ma who was clutching a tattered cup towel to her chest. He felt sorry for the old woman, but he also knew there was no bright future for her daughter here in these hills.

He cleared his throat, "My brother, Mateas, is a preacher, and he'll say the words over us."

In less than an hour Mateas pronounced them man and wife. He had been unwilling to be dissuaded by his siblings. This was for Tavy and the promise he had made him just before he passed. They understood his commitment.

This wasn't much of a sacrifice for Will, really. He'd already made up his mind before Christmas to marry and raise a family in Sweetwater. He just hadn't expected it to come around this way.

With no more discussion on the subject, both families stood in the crowded cabin and watched as Will and Valentine were pronounced man and wife. She was now Mrs. Willheim Brandt, bound to leave these hills with a man she didn't know. The ceremony was short and emotionless.

It was sealed with a peck on the bride's cheek. More loving attention was given to the jug passed around. Everyone took a swig to solidify the union formed between the two families.

Everything had happened in a whirlwind of events. The scratched words reading, "Get my Valentine," gave no hint it referred to a girl. In the end the miscommunication made no difference to Will. A promise made to Tavy was a promise, and he'd keep his word regardless of the consequences.

Valentine's earthly possessions amounted to very little. The items fit into two reed baskets. The contents included a wedding quilt her ma had made a while back, a new apron, a used, cast-iron skillet, and some unfinished piece work. The baskets were put in the back of the small wagon borrowed for the trip to the base of the hills. One of her brothers drove it along with Tavias tucked into a skillfully crafted, wooden coffin made by an old man on the mountain.

The Brandt's rode away from the cabin, and Valen never even looked back. They'd hardly started the decent when her little brother, Winston, darted out from the undergrowth along with Indigo, Red Dog, and Blacksmith at his heels. He approached his sister who was riding in front of Will on his horse.

In his hand he held up the gold watch on the chain Tavy had given to him. He clearly meant to give it to his sister. He wanted her to have it. She reached down smoothing his hair and accepted the offering. She clutched it to her heart smiling with a tear drop rolling down her cheek.

She whispered, "Goodbye, Winston. I love ya."

In Albuquerque, Mateas bought a buckboard from the livery, and Will bought a saddle and tack for a fine gray pony he purchased for Valentine. The sweet, gentle mare had a calm, obliging temperament like hers.

At the general store, Morgan gathered supplies for the trek home. Willheim asked Kat to help the girl pick out a warm woolen coat, hat, new boots, gloves, wool socks, a bandana, two shirts, and a pair of jeans for the chilly ride ahead and because she only had the dress she was wearing.

Will grabbed a fresh bedroll for his wife putting it on the counter along with a hand mirror, a brush, and a comb set. He selected seven hair ribbons, one for each color of the rainbow, a pair of sewing scissors, a package of needles, thread, buttons, and enough calico to make two dresses.

On a whim he picked up a small book of poetry with pictures, selected several candies, and on top of the pile he put a rose scented bar of soap, and a bottle of rose scented cologne. The clerk wrapped everything but the bedroll in brown paper bundles tied with twine. He paid for all the purchases including Val's new clothing she was wearing.

Outside, his brothers had loaded supplies for the trip home into the wagon. He tied the bedroll behind the saddle of the gray mare and tucked the bundles into her saddle bags. When the two ladies came out onto the sidewalk, the men took notice of her with appreciative and encouraging words. She timidly smiled at their praise.

CHAPTER 26

ONE LAST TIME

~Willheim Brandt

It was the destiny of every West Texas cowboy to take a final ride home and for Tavy Brandt, this journey came too early for such good man.

Sunshine had temporarily chased away the harsher elements of the storm blown in from the north. The crispy, breezy air had a stinging bite, and no one could forget winter was still very much in control. It would reign as it pleased until seeds of new growth could be planted in the fields marking the arrival of spring.

The cowboys knew of lonesome trails leading away from Albuquerque, Texas to their homeplace. The little caravan would meander like the crows fly shaving off as many miles as possible. Morgan scouted ahead picking the best routes for Mateas to drive the buckboard carrying Tavy's body.

Mateas's horse was tied onto the back of the wagon, and Katrina followed behind him. Riding together, Will and

Valen brought up the rear. Will felt a profound responsibility toward the girl Tavias had so loved. He also felt apprehension at what he'd done.

Hauntingly, the girl's face showed no signs of emotion, neither sorrow nor peace. She voiced neither an opinion, request, nor a complaint. He knew still waters could run very deep.

Will tried to watch over her through the eyes of his heart. Valentine must be hurting like himself. They'd both been brought together by Tavy's death. He wondered how she was coping with the changes of the past few weeks. Her life had been turned upside down more than once. There had been so many earth-shattering changes. She and Tavy were betrothed to each other before he disappeared.

Her quiet stillness was more deafening to Will than hysterical screams. It cried out to him for help. He was humbled by Valentine agreeing to marry him in Tavy's place, but his feelings didn't stop there. He had a yearning to help her.

He was not a mind reader and wasn't any good at guessing what she was thinking. Anguish filled his thoughts with so many questions, having no answers. He begged God to show him how to improve things for her.

His stomach dipped whenever he thought he witnessed her sorrow in a hesitancy to move or awkwardness with the unfamiliar. He knew learning to be comfortable with her new family and being able to trust them wouldn't happen overnight. It was going to take time and patience for this to work.

Willheim bore the weight of his wife's wellbeing and was wisely focusing on resolving the immediate problems he noticed first. Valentine was too frail, so he was determined she had plenty of food at meals. He also stocked a coat pocket with fruit, beef jerky, rich pemmican, and peppermints to share with her.

In Albuquerque, he had outfitted Valentine with warm

clothing for the cold trek ahead. Mateas helped him pick out the sweet gray mare to ride. She wasn't toughened to the rigors of traveling such a long distance, and he watched for signs of fatigue.

On the back of her gray mare, she looked like an angel. Tavias picked his woman well, and Will felt like a trespasser. This was his brother's rightful love story, but fate intervened to rip it away from him.

He had to keep telling himself Val was his wife, and he was her husband. He had inherited his brother's shy beauty for better or worse, forever and ever, and she had inherited him. He vowed to do right by the gift and the trust Tavias had for him.

Mrs. Willheim Brandt, what a treasure to receive. My brother, you were cheated, but I promise to love and cherish your dream.

Tavias set this all into motion when, under attack and against all odds, he'd hurriedly scratched the message. Then, he had passed it off to Winston, a boy who could neither read nor write. It was by divine intervention it had ever reached Will.

The memory of Tavy sacrificing his dying breath to beg Will to save his Valentine was heartbreaking. At the time, Will had no idea what he was really promising his older brother, but even if he'd understood, it wouldn't have made any difference. For Tavy, he would do anything!

The caravan had not been moving any faster than Mateas could respectfully manage the buckboard. All the while he sang hymns low in his rich voice adding to the backdrop of their mission. An hour before sunset, Morgan chose the sight of their first camp. The horses were tended and a fire laid to provide light, warmth, hot food, and to keep critters away during the night.

Kat encouraged Valentine in a one-sided conversation. The two stepped away together to take care of their personal business, when necessary, away from the men. His eyes followed them until they were out of his sight. The human compassion he felt for Val was great. She was here with people she did not know.

The men cooked a generous hot supper followed with a treat of canned peaches. They sat together afterwards and sipped black coffee together until the large granite pot was emptied.

The stock was checked, and the fire banked with wood they'd gathered before supper. It would last well into the night. Bedrolls had been spread close around its heat. Saddles laid at one end of each to serve as head rests.

Before they called it a night, Morgan said, "Be ready to leave in the morning after breakfast. Pa has received our telegram by now, and he'll be watching the road anxiously for us to ride in with, our brother' Tavy."

Mateas closed with scriptures from the Bible and assured Valentine again she was welcome in the family. He offered a prayer, followed by amens all around.

Will retrieved the worn quilt Val left the cabin wrapped around her this morning. It had been put in the wagon after he bought her wool coat and other warm things. After she lay down, he spread the thick coat over her for added insulation and put the older quilt on top. His own bedroll was by hers in case she needed something in the night.

As soon as camp settled with the rhythmic sounds of sleeping, Will leaned over from his bedding to check on his girl. He had something he wanted, no, something he needed to say to her.

"Are you still awake, Valentine?" he whispered.

Seeing her eyes open, he continued. "Life changing things beyond our control have happened really fast. These things have pushed us together. We're both the same people we were and yet, our paths are one now.

We're both in shock but will adjust to this new order of things if we work together. It's already easy for me to see why my brother loved you so much.

"I can't know what you're thinkin', but I want to tell ya I consider us a team working on the same side of the fence. I'll take care of ya, and you'll be safe with me 'n' never go without. We both just need some time to get comfortable with each other.

"Don't be afraid 'cause I won't rush ya or hurt ya. Tavy would tell you the same about me if he could. I expect nothing from you, Valen, but I'll provide everything ya need 'til you're ready to have me. Do you understand, Val?

"I swore ta my brother I'd find ya and take ya with me to his people. Marryin' ya was the only way ta keep my promise, but I was glad to do it. We'll go slow and sort the details out as we go. It'll be alright, you'll see.

"Don't fret yourself on none of it. We'll find our way ta each other. You rest now; we've got another hard day in the saddle tomorrow."

Gently, he smoothed the quilt anew and touched her soft, wet cheek with his finger. Only then did he notice the watch catching a reflection of light from the fire. She was holding the chain of Tavy's gold watch in her fist. Will saw her clearly through the eyes of his heart.

She was suffering the loss of someone she loved just as he was. Out of empathy, he lightly kissed her forehead. This impulsive gesture surprised him, but it felt right.

Will sat on his bedroll by the fire while he smoked an Ole Shenandoah Cheroot, the best cigarillo wrapped in brown tobacco leaves a cowboy could buy. He heard Valentine shifting under the weight of the covers.

Sleep tight, my girl. I'll build a house, and we'll build a family of our own and raise horses, I think. Life will be good. I promise ya won't be sorry.

CHAPTER 27

ONLY JESUS

~Valentine Brandt

Valentine's memories of Tavias and the future plans he had for them both comforted and tortured her equally. He'd told her all about his family and his papa, and she knew about the farmland waiting for them.

He was going to marry her, build a house, grow crops, and raise a house full of kids. As it turned out, none of those plans were possible. He was dead now.

She'd only known Tavy for a month before he spoke for her. Pa had a price; he always had a price for everything. Without batting an eye, Tavy met the terms. Pa only saw his boys in terms of working them to the bone and his girls as property for sale or trade.

He was a crude, hard man who enforced his rules with a belt or a stick. She couldn't wait to leave her fear of Pa behind her. She was physically afraid of him and afraid for her ma and her two sisters. He preyed upon the helpless.

The last time she saw Tavy, the man she was pledged

to marry alive, he was walking away to hunt game for their wedding feast. Elijah and Winston, her two favorite brothers, went along with him. She was stitching together pieces for a pretty quilt to put on the bed in the house he was going to build. She had never felt so joyous in her whole life!

At least she was gloriously content until the moment Winston rushed in the door bawling, squalling, and in a panic.

"Pa, ahhh, Pa, they's tooked, the ranger man wif guns got 'im, but Tav got me let loose! Got here fas'as I cou'd! I did."

Poor Winston said all these crazy words in practically one breath. He nearly collapsed from the need of air. He'd run all the way back to the cabin and couldn't have made it much farther without collapsing.

Once it sunk into her brain he was talking about Elijah and Tavias, she quietly slipped into her corner and hid behind the spread. She had a dark premonition this was the end of all hope. She cried and trembled without making a sound.

She'd never lain with a man before him. One night when the moon was just a sliver, she and Tavy stole away as soon as the cabin filled with raucous snores. Sneaking around made her afraid Pa would catch them outside, but it made her feel excited too. She trusted Tavy to protect her.

Once he started kissing her, the kisses got longer and sweeter than ever before. A whole other type of excitement sparked through her body, tingling from the top of her head to the tips of her toes. His hands roamed gently, caringly, lovingly beneath the folds of her dress. Tavy's gentile caresses replaced trepidation with feelings too good to be true.

Their bodies coming together was nothing like hearing Pa groping Ma roughly in the blackness of the night. He often slapped her and talked bad making her cry out. She often begged him to stop, but he never listened.

Tavy's touches were different though. His hands were soft and respectful like his kisses. They made her feel cherished, and loved, and beautiful. Except for a pinch of pain, she welcomed him when he entered her body. She felt his seed being delivered, and it made her feel like she belonged to this wonderful man.

The journey north with her love's casket in tow made Valentine miserable, heartbroken, and scared all over again. She was given no choice but to follow the man who looked like Tavy, but he wasn't her Tavy. Now, she was caught up in a knot of strangers, but truthfully, nothing could have stopped her from leaving her pa.

She felt guilty to be happy to finally be free from her pa. It was comforting he wouldn't be able to find her. She was grateful in her heart to Will Brandt for saving her when Tavy couldn't. All of Valentine's contrasting feelings were so totally confusing to her.

Paralyzing sorrow hit her every time she pictured Tavy's body locked in the gloom and isolation of the narrow box. How could he be lying so close and yet so far away from her? Loneliness and desperation made her want to pry the lid open and breathe life from her body into his.

She knew only Jesus was capable of performing such a miracle. He had done it to a man named Lazarus, who had lain in a tomb four days straight as dead as a door nail.

Tavy, my love, I wish you were here. I wish Jesus would put his hand on you. I wish you would rise again.

Chapter 28

Reaching Papa's Home

This arduous journey was almost over. An additional black cloud of dread was forming to join the one already hanging over Valentine's head. When they collided, she was afraid she would burst open.

First, she would have to face Tavy was never coming back and watch his body be buried in the dirt. At the same time, she would come face-to-face with the rest of the Brandts. Valentine couldn't bear the judging stares of flatlanders. She longed for her tiny corner hidden behind the spread.

On the bright side, this was the last night she'd lie on the cold ground wrapped in a bedroll. The thought of being warm again was a welcome thought. Never being under Pa's wrath again was a good thing, but what if Willheim turned out to be just as mean as her pa?

The devil she knew might be better than the one she didn't. Tavy's brother had been kind to her so far, but he hadn't gotten drunk as a skunk yet either. So far, she kept her mouth shut and avoided angering him. Sooner or later though, he was going to get mad about something and show how things were really going to be.

She had no idea what tomorrow was going to bring. Mostly, she didn't know if her heart had the courage to bury Tavy. Without him, she was alone.

There is Will, but I don't trust him yet.

Valentine's fairytale had dissolved in the wind before it even got started. The dreams Tavias had promised her were long gone in the wind. The unknown frightened her. Willheim Brandt may look like his brother, but he wasn't him. People were not interchangeable like shirts.

Val had always hated the hill country dialect. Even to her own ears, her words sounded ignorant, so she stayed silent or whispered as much as possible. Her words and expressions were a stark contrast to the language Tavy used, but it was easy to open up with him. He didn't seem to care, and she had talked freely to him, and he had listened.

His attention made her want to emulate the way he talked. His stories from his life below the hills had given her a tiny glimpse of his world. She hadn't known she could leave the hills until he offered to take her to his home in the flatland.

After he was killed, and his brother spoke for her in his stead, Valentine decided the best defense was to keep silent, listen carefully, and try to learn the sounds of the flatlanders. She had a lot to learn from them. She appreciated it when Kat tried to pull her into conversations. Mateas kindly asked her questions and waited quietly for her faltering answers.

Will spoke to her encouragingly, but she only acknowledged him with sparing words in return. She became nervous and tongue tied around him. On this trip he'd seen her comfort and kept her warm. He especially asked her to eat more. She did the best she could to oblige him, but her body was used to her eating sparingly.

At the store, he bought candy, pretty female trifles, and new, warm clothes for her to wear. The gray pony came as a huge surprise. No hill man would give his woman a horse to ride! He'd expect her to walk or ride double on a mule. Over and over, she remembered what he had said to her.

"Ya like this little gray mare? Mateas helped me pick just tha right pony fer ya to ride. This sweet horse is yers to keep, Valentine. She belongs to ya, but she doesn't have a name 'til you give her one. The best name is only something you can give her."

Valentine had no idea what to think about such a special gift. Ducking her head, she raised her eyes and smiled up at him shyly. She whispered, "Think, ye."

When she spoke those two quiet words of gratitude, he grinned and dipped his head down to her in return.

"Well, Valentine, yer worth is way more than any pony, but she'll do fer now."

In the afternoon, the caravan made it into Papa's yard, and they were greeted by Will's dogs. They had beaten them home. They boiled out of the barn barking. The noisy commotion pulled people out onto the long porch.

As soon as one person's eyes landed on what Mateas was hauling, it seemed like all of them focused in the same direction at once. Everyone walked slowly and silently forward as if they were of one mind.

The family stood to one side silence and waited as Morgan and Mateas loosened the cords holding the tarp in one place covering Tavy's coffin. Then the two brothers pulled it away and folded it neatly.

They stared speechless at the pine box as if their eyes could penetrate the wood to reveal its contents. Whispers about the fine craftsmanship were shared. A lovely carved ribbon was stretched out by two birds and a third hovering above it.

Finally, an old man came forward and a path was cleared respectfully for him. Valentine assumed this was

Papa. He reached over and placed an open hand on the wood. He left it there with his head bowed for several minutes. No one breathed a sound.

Finally, he lifted up his tired, gravelly voice to speak.

"Welcome home, Son. Your journey is over at last. We've all been here waitin' for you."

Those unpretentious words were all it took to break the spell. Men together lifted the casket and carried it carefully to rest on the sawhorses already sitting on the covered porch for this very purpose.

One-by-one, each person, even the children, laid hands upon it. Some said loving words, some shed tears, and others did both.

Willheim and Val took their turn together last, and both wept after Valen said, "I'll luv ye pow'rful ferever, Tavias."

Then Will said, "Goodbye, Ole' Son. You were always a good brother 'n' friend. I kept my promise 'n' brought yer Valentine home, and I'm glad I did. Adios. God's speed ridin' tha green grass trails of heaven."

It was as if a damn had broken, and tears flooded down his face. It took a few moments for him to wipe them away. Then he took Valen's hand, turning them to stand in front of the coffin to face the kin. They were all staring at the yellow-haired girl in their midst whose presence was as yet unexplained.

The group quieted when Will cleared his throat and held up his hand to talk.

"Ya'll this is Valentine Brandt. She's my wife though Tavy had spoken for her before he was killed. He asked me ta bring 'er home. He counted on ya'll ta be good ta her, and I know ya will be. I promised Tavias I'd bring 'er home to the family and take care of her."

Soft mumbles like a gentle breeze shuffling through the papery cottonwood trees fluttered through the air dissipating as if the whispers had never happened.

Willheim continued, "Valentine and Tavy were in love and planned to marry, but they never got the chance.

"I held him in my arms before he took his last breath. He made me promise to bring the love of his life home with me.

"Mateas married us under the eyes of God. Mr. Saxton, her pa, wouldn't agree to let her leave with me otherwise. So, we have taken our vows, and Morgan, Mateas, and Katrina were our witnesses.

"Embrace her wholly as one of us 'cause she truly is a Brandt. We're gonna build a life together and raise a family. I believe Tavy's looking down right now and rejoicing his Valentine is under our protection."

There was only a pause of a few seconds before Meta Anna stepped forward. She hugged both of the newlyweds. Then she said to Valentine, "You belong on this land with us, Valentine Brandt. You are our sister-in-law now and one of Papa's daughters."

Each family member in turn embraced the couple and welcomed Val home before filing one-by-one into the warm house. Tavy's coffin was left where it sat to keep his body from warming. Kat and Savannah brought out a quilt of many colors their mother had made and lovingly draped the cover over it.

Tonight, the men would build a fire outside for coffee and warmth. They'd sit together with Tavy through the night. Tomorrow afternoon, he would be laid to rest in the family cemetery along with his mama as was fitting.

After supper, Willheim and Papa sat alone and talked for a spell in front of the hearth. Will told the whole story to this wise man. Papa puffed on his pipe and listened without interruption until the tale was spent.

"Son, the way I see it you made an honorable move stepping up to marry Valentine like you did. Of course, you remember hearing your mama and I didn't meet until the day of our wedding.

"Our papas had arranged our marriage. It was not uncommon in those days. Everything turned out, and I wish she was still sitting here with me today. Getting to know each other mostly comes later in any marriage.

"You, Tavias, and Kat grew up, side-by-side, like three peas in the same pod. I can understand how determined you were to keep the promise you made to him.

"What are you planning to do now, Son?"

"At tha time, my thoughts were too focused on getting' her out of those hills. I didn't think on anything else. Tha complications of tha situation never hit me until we were headed for here. I felt responsible to protect Valentine any way I could.

She didn't object and I never thought to ask her what she wanted. I should have, but I saw the dangerous conditions she was livin' under.

"Papa, the truth is she had nothing to her name, not even the barest necessities. I bought her warm clothes, shoes, and a horse to make this trip. Val hadn't ever owned a hairbrush, mirror, or any other such things women want. With Kat's help, before leaving Albuquerque, I made sure she had what she needed.

"On the trail, her tears dripped large drops of sadness. In her sorrow she reminded me of a little bird with a broken wing. I did my best to comfort her while working through my own sadness. She had no meat to spare on her bones, so I saw to it she ate her grub before I ate mine.

She rarely spoke, so I talked to her anyway. I threw my bedroll close to hers in case she needed me in the night, and I rode all the way here beside her. Valentine's well-being has become more important to me than my own.

"Am I fond of her? Yes. Am I in love with her? No, but I think I will be given time. She surely is a pretty little thing.

"I've been wondering how she feels and pondering if I should give her a chance out of this marriage. I have not compromised her virtue in any way, but I can't hide her. The neighbors will hear who she is at the funeral tomorrow."

"Son, listen to me, if you're truly thinking on putting her aside, then not one soul around these parts can know the two of you are married.

"A dissolution of matrimony between a man and a wife is a grievous act. It would be shameful to Valentine, to Tavy's memory, to you, and to this whole family.

"This young woman has done nothing to deserve being cast off. Consider what is best for her? Search your heart and follow it, Will. What do you want?"

"Papa, I'd already decided to get married before all this happened. I just hadn't found the girl yet. To tell you the truth, I'm glad we're married. I'm already gettin' used to the idea."

"Willheim you've come this far. You got her out of those hills for Tavy. I'd say he'd be proud you two are together.

"In my opinion, Willheim, you're a married man 'til death do ya part."

CHAPTER 29

THE WAKE AND THE MORROW

~Will

Winter temperatures had allowed the time to get Tavy's body home for a proper burial to give the family closure. Since he was being buried tomorrow, the men of the family were honoring him with a traditional wake tonight. A wake was the one last human interaction with the dead before burial. Stories of their memories of Tavy would be shared.

The vigil would be held all night near where the casket sat on the porch. The cowboys were veterans at braving the cold, but the frigid air posed too much of a risk to Papa's health. Sitting close by the fireplace in the house dozing off and on would suffice for his participation.

He'd be able to see the flames of the bonfire through the windows. His boys would keep it burning all night to warm by and to keep a pot of coffee hot. It was dark now, and the house was quiet since the women and children had already gone to bed.

Well after midnight, Will heard a faint rustle on the

south side of the wrap around porch. He didn't think much on it, until he heard it again. A second bottle of red eye whiskey was being passed back and forth, so no one else noticed the noise but him.

He quietly got up and walked around the corner of the house and almost bumped into Valentine. She was wearing her wool coat and gloves, and her face, tracked with tears, was flushed with the cold.

"Valentine, Honey, how long have you been out here. I wish you'd told me. You're freezing. Come sit with me and feel the heat from the fire. I'll pour you a cup of coffee, and we'll share a quilt."

She nodded her head once in compliance. He felt her shivering and hugged her closer. Once settled, the two sat for a long time with Will's arms wrapped tightly around her under the cover. After a while, he heard her say something but couldn't quite make the words out.

"What did ya say, Valentine?"

"I want ta think ya fer givin' Little Dove to me. She's purty."

"Oh, Valen, someday I'll give ya somethin' better. It's gonna take us both time to grieve Tavy's death. This has been a hard blow, but then I'll court ya proper."

He caressed her cheek and kissed her forehead, and she leaned into him.

Before daybreak, she nodded off and jerked herself awake. He cradled her in his arms and carried her up the stairs. He tucked her into bed before he returned to the porch where he'd left the others.

Ely had made arrangements for the preacher and spread the word of Tavy's internment at the Brandt homeplace. It turned off to be a bitterly cold, windy day, but the sun was bright. A sizeable crowd of friends joined the Brandts, and the women brought food for the funeral dinner.

Meta Anna, Katrina, and even Valentine carved a

cured ham brought in from the smoke house. They'd baked bread and pies. Eggs were boiled, and jars of green beans were opened, and potatoes were peeled and boiled. The community women helped. More hands made for lighter work.

The women Valentine worked beside were pleasant and helpful. In the process of cooking, she had reasons to talk with others and use their names. She began to relax, smile, and even laugh with them. As she began to realize the country women had no intention of treating her poorly, Valentine's confidence in herself began to take delicate roots.

She heard several different accents from people she met on the day of the funeral. Apparently, being different wasn't a reason to feel shame or fear. Many in Texas had immigrated from different places. Val found herself a little more open to trusting people. She wasn't the only one different.

Mateas was kind and comforting, so she sought him out. He was manning a fire outside for brewing coffee to share with whomever wanted it. She watched for Will whenever he was near, and it wasn't awkward to be around him.

Savannah and Kat had quickly altered a dress for her to wear to the service today. They told her there were other items of clothing in the trunk she could wear later with a few alterations. For today, Meta dug to the bottom of the chest and found a pair of black slippers, and the shoes fit well-enough.

When the five Brandt ladies were dressed and descended down the stairs, it signaled the funeral procession was ready to begin. Mateas and Papa drove the wagon bearing the coffin. Willheim, escorting Valentine, walked behind it.

The preacher dressed in black with a white collar rode his mule behind them. Morgan escorted Katrina and next was Meta Anna's family and Savanah with her husbands and children. Friends and neighbors brought up the rear.

They walked eastward to the family cemetery which was less than a mile away. Voices were lifted in songs, "Shall We Gather at the River, "In the Sweet By and By," and "Will the Circle Be Unbroken." Inside the graveyard at the place prepared by friends to receive the treasured remains of Tavias Martain Brandt, Mateas led the gathering in a prayer as melodious sounding as the songs they had sung.

The minister followed by reading text from the Book of Luke. He told stories reflecting what kind of man Tavias Martin Brandt had been. His gentle spirit, and his love of Jesus had been witnessed by all the friends and neighbors in attendance.

After the carved box was lowered gently into the ground on ropes, and the first handful of dirt was thrown in by Papa, Valentine's knees buckled, and she slumped in a faint.

Will scooped her up before she hit the ground and carried her to the wagon. She came around soon enough but did not regain her composure or strength. After the service she was tucked into bed with hot tea and honey.

The guests paid their respects, ate their fill of dinner, and congratulated Will on his marriage before heading back to Sweetwater. Will was relieved when the last family road away.

He thought to himself.

Yes, I'm married to a stranger who belongs to my deceased brother! How is this going to play out?

Of course, Will would never express his frustration out loud, and he chastised himself for even thinking it silently to himself. He felt guilty such a thing had popped into his head. He was partial to Valentine, and Tavy trusted him to take care of her. His thoughts didn't reflect his true feelings. He was just tired and sad. Everything between

Valentine and him would work out.

The family helped each other to clear and put away food. Will took a plate up to Valentine. He knocked on the door, opening it a crack to peek in. He saw her sitting on the side of the bed looking pale. He sat the plate on the little walnut side table and sat down beside her. He began the speech he'd been practicing in his head.

"Valentine, we've got to talk. From where I'm sittin' we're married no matter how it happened. We belong to each other now. Are you handlin' it okay, Val?"

She brought her hand to rest on his forearm, and said, "Will, I know we're married, 'n' I'm good with being yer wife.

"I jest worry might be ye havin' trouble with tha idee. Are ya sorry?"

He looked at his yellow-haired girl and chose not to respond to what she said at the moment.

"What I don't want, Val, is you bein' scared a me. It's like I told ya on tha trail, I don't expect nothin' from ya. I want ya to have time to grieve fer Tavy. I know ya love 'im 'n' I'm glad ya do.

"Valentine, we'll have our time in tha sun. We just gotta let things simmer for a while. Yer wrong 'bout one thing, Valen, I'm not troubled'bout bein' married to ya. Tha fact is I'm really glad we are married, but I don't plan to sleep with ya 'til we're both ready.

"I brought ya food. Ya better try and eat somethin' from this plate. Rest 'n'and build yer strength. Yer light as a feather, and ya don't look a bit well. It's okay ta take some time."

~Valentine

Will left, and Val tried to eat a bite or two, but her stomach rolled, and she spit the bites into the napkin. She finally had to face the fact she was carrying Tavy's child. She'd figured as much the first time morning sickness hit her. She'd seen her own mother, aunts, and cousins at the onset of pregnancies. They were sick at their stomachs just like this.

She had to wait for the best time to tell Will about this baby. This babe wasn't from Will's seed for certain. She had never lain with any man but Tavy. Carrying his child felt right to her, but she feared Willheim might not like it.

Will is very much alive, and Tavy is still living through his child.

Valentine liked Will's sisters. They treated her well and helped her fit in here. She watched, listened, and learned everything she could from them. She intended to make her husband proud of her.

The sisters kept their promise to help her alter garments she could wear from the trunk. She was good at sewing herself. She had the two pieces of flowery calico, needles, threads, sewing scissors, and pretty ribbons Will had bought for her in Albuquerque.

She planned to make the calicos into dresses she could easily make bigger as her belly grew. She asked Meta to show her how to make a pattern, but she didn't tell her why she needed it, exactly.

Val wasn't dull minded by any stretch of imagination. When she set her mind to something, she could be downright stubborn. Nobody worked harder around the place than she did. She charmed the chickens into laying more eggs. She milked the milk cows, and they gave more milk!

One of the barn cats became her special pet. Will's dogs learned to come to her whistle, and she spoiled them rotten. She tended to Little Dove herself and rode her almost every day. She held her own around the kitchen, washed clothes, and cleaned the house. Best of all, she learned to laugh.

The three Austin children adored her and began calling her Aunt Val. She played games with them and enjoyed hearing their stories. She told her own yarns from the hills, and the sharing pleased her. In turn, the children taught her letters, numbers, reading words, history, and geography. Valentine was eager to soak up any kind of knowledge.

Will still hadn't made husbandly advances toward her, which was fine considering her secret. It didn't even seem right to her. It wasn't a problem, because most of the time she wasn't even sure Will was aware of her. He was always kind but nothing beyond general politeness. Their relationship had morphed into nothing more than two passing ships.

Kat still shared a bed upstairs with her sister-in-law, Kat. He continued to sleep by himself on the parlor floor. Val supposed it wasn't any harder than sleeping on the ground. No one asked questions about their relationship. Val resigned herself to their separation. It simply was what it was. At least she was on flatland.

Chapter 30

Something Has to Change!

~Willheim

Willheim's soul ached over the death of Tavias. Everything around him was a reminder of his brother. He had so many good memories of the trouble they used to get into, the laughing, the games, hunting, and the juvenile secrets.

Then there was the pressure of suddenly becoming the man who married Tavy's sweetheart.

In an attitude of depression, it was easier to ignore Valen, but in the throes of his melancholy Will didn't really pay attention to much of anything or anyone around him. He kept an eye on Val from a distance. He was satisfied she was keeping busy, the family loved her, and thankfully she was finally putting on some weight.

For lack of something to do, Will dove into helping Nick on the farm with a vengeance. He didn't like farming and had no desire to be a farmer, but it kept him from thinking too much. The backbreaking, mindless, never-ending, dirty work rendered him too tired by the end of each day to share many words with Valentine or even to eat supper with her.

Will convinced himself she needed this time and space to grieve in peace. In truth, he was staying away from the girl for selfish reasons. It troubled him he had benefited from the death of his brother. Everyday his attraction for Valentine grew stronger, and guilt was eating him up inside.

Dammit Tavy! Did you know I'd have to marry your gal to save her?

The dull ache in his muscles at the end of every workday wasn't quite enough self-punishment to ease his conscience.

Why couldn't I have got to Tavy before it was too late? He should be here and married to Valentine!

Trying to feel even less physical comfort, he started pitching his bedroll on the hard, unyielding parlor floor. Still the extra stress at night wasn't enough added penance to ease his guilt. He only became more discontented and restless.

During one particularly rough night, Elizabeth Hartley came to him in a troubling dream wearing the beautiful cameo he'd foolishly given to her. Visions of her lying under him and every other man in the territory who'd tumble her were disturbing. Being any man's sweetheart for a price was crude and a despicable way to make a living. When he awoke, he was perspiring, angry, and disgusted.

A lot of water had run under the bridge since Lizzy. Her beauty faded considerably as if she had been nothing. He was lucky to have played with fire and not burned. He woke up regretting she had invaded his mind.

I've got to get busy on getting my life together and start building for the future! Something has got to change. It seems like a lifetime ago I was content to just be a cowboy pushing other men's cattle up the trails.

Chapter 31

Buy Me Two Horses

March dawned with spring right around the corner. There were more warm days mixed in with the fewer blustery, cold days now. It was a seesaw of temperatures. The stock was thriving in it, and cows were dropping calves. Meta Anna was spring cleaning and airing the house out.

Will could barely resist the old pull of joining a cattle drive and heading north. Riding off into the sunset and leaving the tension behind would be so easy to do, but he'd never have freedom from his responsibilities again. He was a married man now and would stay put with Valentine.

His brothers and Katrina were set on quitting the trail life too. They were all settling down at the same time. Morgan had been courting a widow woman with a young boy and a little girl since the first of the year. She lived southeast of Sweetwater on some acreage with a sturdy house on her place. He'd move there when they married and still be close enough to farm the land Papa had put aside for him.

Mateas was pastoring in the small black community

near Walnut Grove. The family pitched in with his community to help him raise a sizable one-room cabin in Walnut Grove. He was already living there less than fifteen miles away from Brandt land. He was going to farm his land here.

Will knew Kat was planning to leave again as soon as things got good and green. She was going to check on the elephant one last time. This winter she wrote stories for the Penny Dreadfuls. She also continued to write articles about western life for the newspapers back east and still took photographs to send to the newspapers too.

Kat was a good hand working cattle and horses. She was helping Ely and Papa here on the farm along with Will at the present. He passed a canteen of tepid water to her while they rested from chores in the shade of an ancient cedar. He took this break to run an idea by her.

"Sis, ya have a valuable way with horseflesh. Why, I 'member when we were kids, and I watched ya talkin' horses into doing whatever you wanted. Sometimes you taught 'em ta do things they didn't hanker to do! You most always won them over in the end.

"Buckeye sure cared for ya when we were under fire in tha battle at Jack Helt's camp.

"WHOEEE!

"He was incredible! I don't understand how in the world ya go 'bout teachin' a hard-headed, oversized stallion to stick close as a tick 'n' take care of ya like Buckeye does."

"Yeah, Buckeye is a smart one. He's saved my bacon several times, Will."

"Kat, I been thinkin 'bout y 'n' me throwin' together to build a horse ranch. I'm serious. Both of us together have enough land to do it. I doubt yer plannin' on bein' a farmer, n' I'm sure not!

"I can round up mustang herds 'n' get 'em back here, green break 'em, 'n' doctor 'em too. We'll do our own hoof trimin', n' shoein'. We can buy good mares for breeding. I bet Buckeye'd be all for helpin' us out.

"Why, tha two a us both have experience with horses, and I betcha we can sell a few for top dollar. I know 'bout the aspects of tha horse business. What I don't know is tha way ya have a gettin' inside a horse's head. It's a special gift.

"Ahhh, I can take a wild bronc 'n' make it a dependable saddle horse. I can take one 'n make it be a decent cutter. I can train horses to be ropers, heelers, 'n' headers, but I don't have yer special gift fer training the way ya do, Lit'l Sister. You were born with it."

She laughed, "Brother, are you trying to butter me up with all these sugary words? Don't worry, I was all in when you said horse ranch!

"Horses as smart as Buckeye are hard to find. I saw one like him on the Rio Grande close to Laredo. He was a huge stallion called Big River owned by a woman rancher by the name of Ruby.

We both considered it was possible Buckeye and Big River were from the same bloodline. Her pa raised horses. One day bandits attacked and stole his whole string and murdered her folks. She was just a child but managed to save herself, a little brother, and one little colt, Big River.

"I'll never forget the day I ran across Buckeye. Two dumb ass wranglers were mistreating him. I suspected right off the stallion might prefer a lighter touch and a soothing voice. It turned out I was right.

"The two fools threw in the towel and labeled him too dangerous. I approached the owner, and he gladly agreed to sell the stallion to me for a paltry sum. He warned me I'd likely get hurt. He didn't have a man who could ride him. He said a fool-woman could get killed.

"I had a hunch about the horse, but I didn't argue. Now, we fit like preserves and biscuits!"

"I worked patiently and consistently earning his trust.

It wasn't too long before he followed me around while I rode another horse. I named him Buckeye and lavished him with attention. He picked up routines quickly.

"The more he learned, the easier he learned. I taught him skills most useful to me. He became protective all on his own."

"Don't give Buckeye more credit than yerself, Kat. I'm not sa sure many can work a horse better than you. With yer talent and my brawn, we're sure to make money!"

After a couple of weeks of hashing the particulars out with Papa and making a workable plan, they formed an agreeable partnership. Papa gave them three bordering shares of land, one for Will, one for Kat, and one for Tavy because of Valentine.

Prior to 1836, Pa received a labor of land, 177.1 acres, for farming. It was distributed through the Stephen F. Austin colony in Texas. After 1836, he received an additional league, 4,428 more acres, because he declared he'd raise cattle.

Later, the Republic of Texas found itself richer in land than funds. Papa and others bought additional land for fifty cents on the acre. The Brandts ended up with quite a substantial parcel. As part of Meta Anna's piece, she was given the original farm plus more. Nick kept it in cultivation and continued to raise cattle. There was plenty to divide evenly among all of Martin's and Matilda's children.

Around the first of April, Katrina left in search of material and photographs to fuel more stories. She was also going to keep her eyes open for good breeding stock.

Willheim was riding south to round up a herd of wild mustangs tomorrow morning to get them started.

Both of them deposited equal amounts of money to stake their joint business. The account was at the bank there in Sweetwater and either partner could draw from it as needed.

Valentine was on the fringes listening to their plans being discussed. The afternoon before Will rode south, she asked him upstairs to talk. She chose her words carefully. Will was shocked to realize she had already lost a good deal of the awkward hill dialect.

When was the last time they'd spoken more than polite acknowledgements to each other? He looked down into her beautiful eyes and silently vowed to court her when he returned from this trip.

Hmmm, Val's gained some weight. I'll thank Meta for seeing she's been eating more.

"I heard yer leavin' in tha morrow to get horses. You 'n' Kat are workin' together, aren't ya?"

He nodded sheepishly. He should have already talked to her about this.

Hesitantly, Valentine spoke again. "I've got a poke put back, 'n' I want ya to take it so I kin be part a tha bus'ness too."

Will could hear determination in her voice.

"Valentine, what amount of money could you possibly have? I didn't know you had any cash. Where'd ya get it?"

She reached into the bosom of her shirtwaist as Will's eyes traced her hand. Until this very moment, he hadn't noticed how full and round her breasts were.

She withdrew a roll of bills from the hollow between them.

"Count it, Will. Tavy gave it ta me tha day he walked away 'n' didn' come back. He tol' me to hold it."

Her lips quivered. She rushed several steps backward to get away from Will while ducking her head sideways and raising her arms protectively. Did she think he was going to strike her?

She shrank further away and cowered lower. The roll of paper money dropped to the floor when both of her hands flew up to shield her face!

She had taken an unmistakable stance of fear. Her

show of panic touched him deeply.

What's happening here?

He immediately closed the space between them and pulled her into his arms. Her body was stiff as a board, but he held her in a crush to his chest. He smelled the delicate scent of roses, probably from the soap and cologne he'd given her.

He couldn't detect any evidence his protective actions were calming her. Slowly and tentatively, he began to stroke her silky hair.

"Yer tremblin', Val. Shhh, now-- don't be afraid a me. Why are you actin' this way?" he asked soothingly in a soft, kind tone. It was the same gentle voice he would use to distract a hurt filly.

She whispered between soft sobs causing the front of his shirt to dampen. He strained, trying to hear what she was saying.

"It come ta me ya might be mad 'cause I kept this money from ya. I should of give it to ya straight away. I knew I should, but it's so special 'cause he give it ta me the last time I saw him."

"Ya mean Tavy?"

"Yeah. If Pa had guessed I had it, he'd a thrashed me fer not handin' it over to 'im. I got scared you was gonna whip me with yer belt fer keepin' it hid."

As if a floodgate had broken, she bawled all the harder.

The abuse was why Tavy asked me to save his Valentine. Tavy hoped I'd love Valentine. He passed her to me, and so far, I've made a mess of things. Tavy, I promise you I'm gonna get this right.

Once the tears started falling, the cloth of his shirt became drenched. She finally cried herself out, relaxing and molding into him like a child. She sobbed and whimpered for a good long while as he continued to hug her snuggly against him saying soft words.

"Cry, Val, cry it all out Sweetheart, cry out all the

misery you've been holdin' in these past months."

Willheim could kick himself for his part in treating her inconsiderately. He'd made an unjustifiable mistake in deciding she was better off suffering alone. He was the one who needed to come to terms with Tavy's death and suffer alone!

He was so quick to direct indignant anger toward her pa for hurting her physically, but he was hurting Val too by ignoring to find out what she really needed from him.

Losing Tavy's love must have pulled the rug right out from under Valentine. Then, overnight she was married to a stranger, albeit the stranger was his brother. Then he whisked her away to a unfamiliar land and handed her over to people she didn't know or understand. How could he have been so dense not to have cared she was overwhelmed? How selfish he'd been to think more about his sorrow and little about Val's loss!

"Valentine, Love, listen to me. I'm not your Pa, and you're not livin' in the hills anymore where women are mistreated. Yer safe here with me and Tavy's family. I'm sorry, more than you'll ever know, for the distance I've kept between us.

"Tavy dying clouded my thinkin', but I'm here with you. You're not alone. We're here now because he put the two of us together!

"I can see you, Pretty Girl, my lovely, precious wife. Believe this, I will never raise a hand to you in anger. You never have to fear me, and if any man dares lay a hand on ya again, I swear I'll kill 'im, I will! You're mine, my pearl to protect, so help me, God!"

He pulled out his bandana and mopped her face and made her blow her nose, twice. Then, he cupped the back of her head and laid tender kisses on her cheeks, neck, and forehead.

He picked the money up and said, "Val, Honey, this money Tavy gave to you is yers. He meant for you and no one else ta have it. It's a gift from his heart. It's special, and I will never take it or anything else you treasure from you."

Valentine looked up at him. "Isn't there enough here, Will, to buy at least two horses. I want you to buy two horses and be a part of the horse ranch with you 'n' Kat. Will, I have to feel like I belong somewhere."

Will sighed and patiently helped her count the money and was surprised at the sum. This had to be most of his brother's spring and fall earnings combined. To satisfy her earnest plea, he took out only enough to cover the price of two head.

"Put the rest of this somewhere safe."

As he was leaving the room, he said, "Valen, you'll always belong here with me. Don't forget it. Give me a little more time to get us a place of our own."

Chapter 32

What Did Ya Say?

After gathering his gear, the next morning and saddling Rope Tail, Willheim stopped by the kitchen to pick up the grub sack Meta Anna would have ready for him. She was standing in the middle of the room with her arms twined tightly across her chest, and her lips clamped firmly in a frown.

Even a blind man couldn't have missed the tension in the air. He didn't know much about women, but he knew this one well enough to see she had a twist in her bonnet.

Will stopped in his tracks and waited for her to take a swing at him. He didn't have to stand there for long before she started picking things up like she was busy and slamming them around like they were important.

She roughly dropped day old biscuits into a five-pound flour sack and dropped it into his larger grub sack along with a hunk of cured bacon wrapped in cheesecloth, a pound of coffee, some canned tomatoes and fruit, and a few other trail friendly foodstuffs.

Carelessly or maybe on purpose, she pushed an iron

skillet off the countertop, and it landed with a rattling clank onto the floor. She stared at Willheim.

"Okay, Sis, tell me tha reason you're so gol-darned mad at me! What'd I do ta so ruffle yer feathers? Make it quick 'cause I need to be leavin'."

Meta cocked a hand on her hip and asked Will sharply, "Don't you have eyes in your head? Surely, you're not the dumbest man in Nolan County?"

When he knit his eyebrows together but didn't answer, she hissed loudly through her mouth drawn up into a knot.

"I'll take your silence as a yes, you are the dumbest man! For how long are you planning to be gone Mr. Willheim Brandt?

"Not until next Christmas, I certainly hope! You have things here needing to be tended, real responsibilities for once in your life, not the made-up kind men like you use for excuses!"

"Why—in—tha—hell are ya sa angry, Meta?" he demanded, raising his voice to match hers.

Right now, his older sister reminded him so much of Ma when she got her dander up. He almost squirmed like a guilty boy again!

"Four, five, six weeks, probably more. It'll take a while to hire vaqueros, find a herd of wild mustangs, round 'em up then get 'em back here.

"Darn sarnit, quit beatin' around the bush, Meta, and use yer words! I need to get on the road. What are these important responsibilities needin' ta be handled? Tell me what's sa important it can't be taken care of later?"

"Men! Ya'll never think of anyone but yourselves!"

"Now, I take offense at yer low opinion a me!"

He squinted his eyes at her trying to figure out why the hell she was fussing so.

"I'm talkin' 'bout Valen, your wife. Remember her, Willheim? She is with child, or haven't ya taken the time to look at her? You make dang sure you're back here quick-like. She's going to be needing her husband, don't you think?

"This is her first baby. You can't leave her to do this without you. It's about time to step up and start acting like her husband for a change. Quit ignoring this gentle girl! I've held my peace for too long if you ask me.

"No Sir, I don't intend to keep quiet anymore. Dammit, you make sure you do the right by her, Mr. Big Cowboy Will, Mr. Big Britches! Mmph!"

Willheim knit his eyebrows together until they met as one in the middle. He was clearly flabbergasted on hearing this news come out of Meta's mouth.

"Well, don't be lookin' at me--we haven't even, well, ya know what I mean. I didn't get her pregnant."

"I assumed as much, Brother, but you did marry her, and you're all she has in this world. Obviously, it's Tavy's baby, I figure, and you're going to be its pa!

"You better get your business done and get back here fast as a roadrunner. Get your life in order. I'll be watching the road for you to come home."

"I'm sorry I yelled at you, Will. You'll have to forgive me, Brother."

Too stunned at the moment, to say anything but understanding Meta Anna being upset, Will nodded his head.

"Believe me, Meta Anna, I didn't know 'bout this 'til ya told me. I'll take care of 'em both, I promise. I'm gonna build a house and do right by both of them."

"I know you hadn't caught on to this yourself, and I know you'll try to do better," she said.

He picked up his grub sack and let the door hit him on the way out.

The brush dogs sensed he was getting ready to move again. They caught the telling-scent of cured bacon he stuffed in his saddle bag before he tied the grub sack to his saddle where he always carried it when he was leaving.

Rope Tail fairly stomped his feet in anticipation of getting on the road again.

Will's mind was circling with the weight of the world on his shoulders as his little troop hit the trail. Before he rode out of the yard, he looked back over his shoulder and saw his yellow-haired girl standing at the upstairs window, watching.

She lifted her hand in a timid wave, and he touched the brim of his hat and dipped his head to her. He smiled, and so did she. He had no idea Valentine stood still watching at the window until he was completely out of sight.

There was a babe growing inside of her, Tavy's baby to be specific. Will was putting in some time chewing on this news. He guessed he was as blind as his sister accused him of being. Heck, he hadn't noticed a darn thing until she pointed the signs out!

Will had so much running through his mind. It was a relief to ride out and leave home behind him for a while. The long jaunt in the saddle from Sweetwater to Mexico came at just the right time.

This new development in his life was the kind of shock a man needed singular solitude to think on a spell. He had felt so confident he had everything under control until now. Oh, how wrong Will had been!

Meta's abrupt revelation about Valentine before he left this morning had hit him right between the eyes. Marrying his brother's fiancé after he died was bound to come with a few tangles, but he sure didn't see the complication of a baby coming.

With every intention of taking care of Val and the baby, he needed time to digest this information. Just a few months ago he had only himself, Rope Tail, and the dogs to keep on track. He needed to breathe freedom for a few days to get his mind wrapped around this.

As a rule, he wasn't a man who relied on liquor for courage, but when Meta Anna raked him over the coals about Valentine's condition, he sure wouldn't have turned down a swig or two of red eye whiskey! It never occurred to him even for a second to doubt his older sister knew what she was talking about.

She'd birthed three young'uns of her own, so he trusted she knew a pregnant female when she saw one. Meta Anna was a downright expert on the subject. What he didn't know about women and babies could fill an empty freight wagon!

The only fact he knew to be certain was it took a man and a woman to make a baby. For sure, he knew this child Valentine was carrying wasn't his. Meta Anna hit the nail square on the head about this too. It didn't take a genius to believe it was his brother's baby.

It was a heady thought considering Tavy was deceased, and yet, a part of him still lived on this earth. Will felt happy Tavy had planted his seed. The babe warming in Val's belly belonged to both brothers now, and he was happy about it.

Boy howdy, Tavias, when you give a gift, it just keeps on giving. I'm not complaining, Brother, but I'm in a quandary as to the best way to handle your trust in me.

Claiming Tavy's woman after he died was natural, and Tavy's begotten offspring fell under the same umbrella of protection. Will's insides dipped and rolled with regret. His older brother had been denied the joys of raising his own son or daughter.

Willheim vowed to God right then and there he would step up and be a husband and a pa worthy of such a valuable inheritance. He'd make sure this child grew up knowing the Lord and knowing Tavy, and he'd love Valentine with his whole heart.

Yesterday, he turned a blind eye to the thickening of Val's waist and the increasing heaviness of her breasts. He had attributed the increases to the powers of good food aplenty and lots of rest. Any other possibility had gone over the top of his head.

It wouldn't be a hardship to take on this little one. Will was already falling in love with the mother. For a while he had been prepared to consummate their marriage vows. With a baby coming, it was imperative to make her his wife in every way.

He had many things to accomplish though. Where would his little family live? A house had to be built. Also, he had to set the plans in motion to support them which was why he was on his way to Mexico. It was the first step to starting the horse ranch. When he got back to Sweetwater, he'd start putting his back to the grindstone.

CHAPTER 33

WILD NED MASON

~*Willheim Brandt*

Before he crossed the Rio Grande at Del Rio to reach the village of Nueva Rosita Will had to take shelter in a thicket of trees for an hour to wait for a thunderstorm to pass through. When he got to the perpetually dirty little town, the dirt streets had been turned into a mire of sticky mud. What a mess!

He came here because this place was known to be where el mesteneros hung out between jobs. Experienced mustang runners could usually be found and hired as mustang salvajes, wild horse wranglers.

He hadn't expected to see anyone he knew, but at the livery stable he ran into Randall Pike. They'd ridden together twice in the past. He had the reputation of being a dependable hand.

Will explained he was investing in a horse ranch and offered him a job, and he readily agreed to sign on with him. He also mentioned a friend here and vouched for him to be a steady-minded cowboy. They easily found him in a noisy cantina drinking red eye and playing a game of cards.

Another man named Xavier, overheard the offer Brandt made and declared he was looking for a job. All Will needed to round up a herd of wild mustangs and drive them north across the Rio Grande was three more vaqueros

Along the way, he'd keep his eyes open for some good-blooded breeding stock to buy. More than once, Will wished Katrina was with him on this trip. He knew he might as well skip wishing. It was purely a waste of time! If a man wished in one hand and shit in the other, he knew which hand would fill up faster.

He couldn't begrudge his little sister answering the call to hit the trail one last time. She needed closure on the lifestyle she'd successfully established. A cowboy or cowgirl had to follow their hearts wherever they led them.

A twinge of insecurity bedeviled him. Picking out horseflesh for their new business venture was a gamble, and Kat was the one with the better intuition when it came to horses.

For the sake of comradery, he treated his three new employees to a thick beefsteak for supper. During table conversation Randall asked Willheim if he remembered Wild Ned Mason.

"Do ya 'member old Wild Ned? Flores only trusted him to provide the remudas for his drives. He didn' wan' any mounts 'ceptin' the ones Ned brought to 'im personal! Flores wus supersteetious 'bout it 'long with a lot a other things as I recall!"

"Yeah, I sure do remember Ole Wild Ned. Wonder whatever happened to 'im? What I wouldn't give ta have tha peculiar old codger on my side a tha fence today! I'm guessing he's probably dead by now since I haven't seen 'im 'n' a couple a years. He could sure weed bad horseflesh out of tha good. I wish I could conjure tha feller out a thin air with the snap a my fingers."

Randall and Xavier threw their heads back and laughed loudly calling attention to their table. Will couldn't understand why his words had struck them as being so funny.

"Well, as it turns out yer conjuring ability is sure powerful. Mason had quite a' eye fer tha ladies as well as tha horses! Sadly, he didn' cere if tha ladies wus married er single. One rancher in 'ticular didn' like 'im messin' with his little senora. He beat the hell out of 'im 'n' about twisted an arm off. He left it bad crippled. It didn' heal straight," said Randall, shaking his head.

Xavier threw in, "Now, iffen yer really serious 'bout findin' tha ole sot, he's hole up 'ere 'n' Nueva Rosita somewheres. He crawls outta his hole ever' once in a while and does a few odd jobs for pocket change. Stays drunk mos' a tha time."

You can bet Will was interested in this news! Dang right, he was.

"Can he still ride and all? I mean, if his legs er alright, he can sit a horse and point out good stock with his one good arm, can't he? We're gonna go find him first thing in the mornin'. I need Ned's expertise on my horse ranch.

"Have another nickel beer on me, Boys!

The next day, it wasn't hard to find the unconscious man. After they asked at the main cantina first and then moved down the street to a smaller one, they hit paydirt!

"Si, I saber el hombre. I kin show ya where he sleeps, but Senor, I'll not be goin'in thees place contigo. Hees malo este hombre 'fore the sun is high, an' eet's too caliente to sleep no mas. Theen, el perro cur drinks to git borracho agin 'til he don' see luz del dia no mas. Is a teerable life ee has aqui con nosotros. Someone needs to put una pistola en la cabeza, put heem outta hees misery, I theenk."

Not put off by her broken English and the character warning, Will and the other two walked through a wide-open doorway into a dim, filthy-smelling adobe room with no window and an uneven dirt floor littered with straw. He waited while his eyes adjusted to the little light let in by the entrance. Heavy breathing and snoring sounded from one side of the musty space.

Three steps toward the sound disturbed a rooster at the end of the cot. The disgruntled bird went squawking and flapping, flying by Will's head toward the door. The commotion roused the sleeping form. A man smacked his lips and snarled obscenities with a thickened tongue.

"Who's there, ya son-uf-bitch? I'll put a bullet 'n yer no good, sorry hide, I swear, jus' leave me 'lone!"

"Wait, hold your fire, Wild Ned. It's Willheim Brandt. Get up! I came ta talk ta ya."

Wild Ned Mason could barely open his bloodshot eyes. To Will he looked older, broken, and more forgotten than wild anymore. It soon became obvious his left arm was mangled and ruined. Will mused he'd been lucky the rancher hadn't shot off his pecker instead of cropping his wing. Either Ned had been a faster runner than he remembered, or the angry husband had only meant to mark him for life.

It took Willheim, Randall, and Xavier a good while to get the old man onto his unstable legs. Then it took longer to get him to talk halfway sensible. His one good hand shook with his craving for rot gut. He needed black coffee and food.

After forcing almost, a full pot of strong coffee down his throat, Will began to assess his condition mentally and physically. If this shell of the man, he'd once known, could be salvaged Will planned to take him out of this town and clear the fog he'd been living in.

They fed him, hired a hot tub with lye soap, got him a shave and a haircut, and put new clothes and boots on his sorry carcass. The air around him smelled a whole lot better, but he was none too enthusiastic about their effort.

By late afternoon, he showed signs of exhaustion and passed out in a rented room. Will sat with him. When the sun went down, Will lit the kerosene lamp and dozed off in a chair. Before morning, Wild Ned opened one eye. He saw the shadow of a cowboy sitting in a chair with his legs stretched out in front of him. His hat was pulled down over his face.

Ned hollered hoarsely, "Who be ye? Whatdaya want from me? I'm waitin' tu die, leave me tu it? Now, I'll have to start dyin' all over agin tomorry, let me see yer sorry face do-gooder! What ere ya, a dadblasted Sundy school teacher?"

Will sat perfectly still in no hurry to speak.

Finally, he said in a slow, steady drawl, "I wouldn't a thought a real west Texas legend of yer fine caliber 'n' skills woulda let 'imself go sa far down. Ya oughta be ashamed fer wastin' away hidin'in this Godforsaken hell hole.

"Where's yer pride ole man? I 'member tha first string a horses I saw ya bring inta Eddy Flores's camp. Ya were a wild 'n' crazy horseman, I wanted ta grow up 'n' be just like ya!

"Who ere ya preachin ta me? State yer name! Whata ya know 'bout me."

"I know ya can't keep yer pecker in yer pants away from a'nother man's wife! My name's Willheim Brandt. 'Member me or is yer brain too far gone?"

"Yeah, I guess I do, ya li'le snip! Ya don't see tu good, do ya? I only have one good arm! I can't do tha work I ust ta!"

"I'll tell ya what I do see alright. I see a man who knows horses, 'n' I see a man I can use on my horse ranch. I see a man who can still sit a horse. I see a man who can use his good arm to point out the best horseflesh in Mexico 'n' Texas!

"Most importantly, I see Wild Ned Mason, the man

I've always admired, he's gonna leave this stinkin' place with me taday to point out the best horses we can find ta herd back ta Sweetwater, Texas. Yer coming home ta work fer me, old man!

The difference in Ned Mason after getting a hand up from a friend was nothing short of a miracle. Will took the whiskey away, dried him out, and cleaned Ned up. The promise of a job began to restore his self-respect and gave him hope.

Will laid down the law to him.

"For starters, there'll be no more drinking. It has to be understood, tha money I've spent on rehabilitating ya, and the horse and tack I bought ya will come outta yer first month's wages.

"Make no mistake, you'll be workin' for my sister and me, but I'll be yer boss. Get it through yer head I'll be callin' the shots startin' taday. While yer workin for me, you'll leave other men's wives alone, or I'll shoot yer other arm off.

"Your first work is ta help me pick out the best wild mustangs we can find and herd 'im to Sweetwater to my spread. I have three hands and three vaqueros who'll be working with us. Ya have ta agree ta stay on with me at least one year.

"If you can agree to all the terms and conditions, I listed, then I'll get ya outta this filthy town. Agree to it all or there's no deal."

"Is that all, Mr. High and Mighty? There ain't nothin' else?" he asked sarcastically.

"Yeah, there's one more thing. My wife and I are in partners with my little sister, Kat. My sister's a sure 'nough horsewoman. She knows her stuff. If Kat tells ya do somethin', then ya do it. Now, what's it gonna be, the job in Sweetwater or a fresh bottle a red eye here."

"Yer right gutsy, Brandt. I got boots older 'n' you! There ere few men could get me ta take orders. Yer treadin' on a thin sheet a ice, but I'll let ya be tha boss. I dang sure ain't gonna take orders from no little baby sister," he countered.

"Nah, this woman's not like yer a thinkin'. She can ride, shoot, fight as good as any man, and nobody trains horses as good as her. I doubt you'll have trouble respectin' Kat once ya get ta know her."

Running his good hand over his whiskers and shakin' his head, Wild Ned held out his good arm to shake on it. The truth was he had nowhere else to go, and he knew Will was giving him a chance to start over.

Wild herds wandered west away from people, and Brandt's men went this way probably costing them a week. They entered the desolate, rough, desert land of Lajitas Mesa which was broken table land with millions of little flat stones. It was hardly even fit for rattlesnakes and chaparrals. Any horse favoring this landscape had to be as strong and self-reliant as the Texas Longhorn.

The crippled drunk, Wild Ned Mason, returned to the living and rose to leadership among the men. Ned hadn't lost his expertise when it came to locating a herd and separating brushtails from the better horseflesh.

Ned still had it in him! Willheim, being a smart man, gladly took a step back and allowed him to ramrod. Ole Ned spoke fluent Spanish with a boy named Emanuel who could lead them to a herd of approximately one hundred and fifty or more for a price, of course.

Wild Ned was quick to point out rounding up a herd of feral animals this size might take some doing. Rattling oats in a bucket might entice domesticated horses to run to you but not so with these fuckers. They'd have to get hold of the lead stallion to get the others to fall into line and follow them.

With a similar loyalty, Will and his men covertly followed Wild Ned crawling on their bellies through the tall dry grass, downwind to get the first glance of the herd.

It was breathtaking to see the horses gathered in coats of many colors with muscles rippling and tails swishing away the flies. Strong looking, solid bodies with long, sleek tails were evidence of heartiness.

All totaled, the horses numbered one hundred and sixty-seven. After visually culling out the brushtails with signs of inbreeding like smaller statures, stragglier coats, and shorter, bushier tails one hundred and thirty was the final count.

A few already wore random brands which meant they'd strayed from wagon trains, outlaws, dead cowboys, or even established outfits. Roaming with a wild herd, they were free for the picking. At the Brandt horse ranch, each horse would wear B, the Lazy B brand.

Will tampered his enthusiasm by contemplating the enormous task ahead. It would test the skills of every cowboy. Ned kept them as close as possible to the herd without letting the human scent be detected. They subtly and cunningly infiltrated the perimeters in well-orchestrated maneuvers.

One of the hired mustang salvajes had isolated himself from the men since crossing the Rio Grande. He had not washed or changed clothes, and food had been tied in a bush or placed each day for him to find. By the end of another week, he was able to relocate up wind of the magnificent, black stallion leader.

Ned had already started gently and with nonintrusive nudging to slowly direct the herd northeast toward Sweetwater. Will had a place with plenty of water and grazing to hold their interest into staying. Before he left home, he had employed a team of fence builders to enclose a large area of his, Kat's, and Tavy's land for this purpose.

It was over a month since Will rode away from Valentine. Meta Anna would just have to forgive him for the delay. A cowboy can't be penned down to a time schedule. Actually, he was itching to get back and start building Valentine's house. He was most anxious to live with her and the child she carried. They were the most important part of his world now.

Chapter 34

Maternal Awareness

~Valentine Brandt

Val was right there in the room when Savannah Grace gave birth to a fine boy. His first cry affected her in a totally unexpected way. The first chirp of the newborn stirred an involuntary response from deep inside of herself, and she felt liquid leaking out from one of her breasts. She looked down and quietly gasped at the spot of moisture she saw. A dampened circle, a shade darker than the cotton of her gray shirtwaist, appeared at the tip of a swollen breast. She hurried to pull her shawl more closely lest someone notice the moisture.

She helped Meta Anna clean up the baby boy while the doctor continued to attend to their sister-in law. Later, as Valentine watched Savannah offer him her nipple for the first time, she felt the sensation again and stepped back farther away.

She watched for a moment as Ely entered the room to see his wife and child for the first time and wondered if

Willheim would ever be so concerned about her. She slipped out and hastily escaped to the bedroom she and Ella shared. She was anxious to clean up and change out of the soiled shirtwaist before anyone could see what had happened.

She knew the new baby and Mother were resting now for entirely different reasons. Savannah was exhausted from the exertion of birthing. Little Seth had a full stomach and was content. Everything was as it should be.

The Brandt family had congregated in the parlor. Everyone was there except Will and Kat. All were joyfully celebrating the beginning of new life as if the occasion was a party. Valentine wondered if they would give her baby such a reception into the world. Would Willheim even bother to be present? She was beginning to doubt it.

How long had it been since she'd seen him? She had overheard Meta and Savannah whispering a few days ago about how long he'd been away. Val believed it was growing more unlikely she and Will would ever be together with each passing day. She began to lean on the memories she had of Tavias for comfort. It wasn't enough to fill the hole in her heart, but it had to be.

Valentine had been living in the Benton home for a while now. When Savannah's time had neared, she had asked Valentine to come. Since Savannah Grace's waist had gotten so bulky, she had slowed down out of necessity and needed help with the work. Being useful had eased much of the emptiness Val felt. She loved the Benton children and had never been so happy as she was here.

The hustle and bustle in town was fascinating. She enjoyed the chores of cooking and washing for the family and felt she had a purpose. Stocking and dusting the shelves in the store, sweeping, and helping customers were exhilarating. The shiny, colorful merchandise was like a king's ransom. Store bought goods had not been a plentiful sight where she'd been raised in the hills.

At the farm, she had made friends with Meta Anna's children. She loved sitting with them when they did their schoolwork around the table. They brought homework from school each day to complete. Valentine soaked up as much of their studies as she could. She had a thirst for learning to read, write, cypher, and speak correctly.

Now she shared the bedroom with sweet Ella, Savannah's oldest. They became good friends quickly. One night, Valentine admitted her shame at being uneducated. Ella began tutoring Val each evening after they went to bed.

Valentine spent every spare minute learning to write, do sums, and read. She caught on quickly, and made great strides in her skills during the weeks Will had gone. Her newfound knowledge and confidence made her an asset in the general store.

The Benton family never mentioned taking her back to the farm after Seth was born, and she didn't dare to mention it either. Valentine was appreciated here and settled into Savannah's family. She'd never had a close friend like Ella in her life, and she cherished their friendship.

She was content, but feelings of being a misfit clouded her self-esteem with doubts in herself. Why would Willheim have left her with his family? If she was suitable, he wouldn't have ridden out and stayed away. A great misunderstanding festered within Valentine's tender heart. She judged herself too inadequate to hold onto a man like Willheim. The idea she was worthless kept growing inside her like a weed.

~*Willheim*

Will's trip into Mexico took more time than he'd figured it would. He worried he was away from Valentine much longer than he should have been. When he finally returned home and discovered his wife was not at the farm waiting for him to return, he was disgruntled. He hadn't expected her to be gone.

Stubbornly, he focused on the work he had to do with building the horse ranch. The mustangs he brought back to be secured, settled, and tended. His hired hands had to have a sturdy bunkhouse with a cooking area. It was the first building to be constructed and where Will stayed too. Then, the barn and corral went up next.

The cowboys abhorred using saws, hammers, and nails. They were insufferable carpenters. If something couldn't be done on the back of a horse, they didn't want to do it at all. They cursed, argued, and complained. They declared loudly they hadn't signed on to be builders.

They mashed their thumbs with hammers among other minor injuries. Their measurements were more often off than inaccurate. Somehow, Will and his men made progress and muddled through until they were finished. It helped immensely Morgan, Mateas, and Nick took pity on him and put in several days to help.

The three cowboys he'd hired in Mexico had thankfully agreed to stay with him for a while. The three Mexican vaqueros were very content with the pay he offered and likewise stayed with him to work the horses.

Ole Wild Ned was quite a surprise. After he dried out and was well-fed, and rested, he got his second wind and regained strength. He quit feeling sorry for his lot in life and rose to meet his legendary status. Will made him the Segundo on the ranch, his second in command.

The old man earned his stature back among the cowboys. Oh, he was still as cantankerous as he'd always been, but his expertise and Will's skills complimented each other greatly. The ranch was taking shape faster than Will had hoped. When Katrina got back, she'd be surprised to find sales were already being made. Once the word got out, men from all around came looking for horses to buy.

Will should have gone into Sweetwater before this to

see Val, but to tell the truth he was hurt by her disappearance. Why would she not have come back home once Savannah Grace's baby had been born?

He took a notion one day to get cleaned up and head into town to fetch Valentine in the buggy. It was time she returned to the farm where she belonged. He was actually excited at the thought of bringing his bride back to Papa's house. How could he take care of her otherwise?

Meta had her nose out of joint with him over the delay, but what else was new? She was always perturbed about something. She chastised him for waiting so long to go get her. Before leaving, he made it clear to Meta Anna he was going to start building Valentine a house on the ranch where they could live together. He'd hired a crew of carpenters and would have the house built right.

He'd already ordered the lumber and window glass, and it would all be delivered any day. He'd get Ely to order a good cookstove, a proper copper bathing tub, and hand pumps today while he was in Sweetwater. He didn't want Valentine to know what he was doing until the house was finished. It would be her wedding gift and ready to move into before the baby was due.

He pulled up in front of Benton's General Store and dropped the twenty-five-pound buggy weight to the ground by its tether to hold the rig in place. Will was suddenly hit with nervousness. Meta was right when she had said he should have already come to see Val. Waiting to come get her was making this more awkward than it had to be.

He entered the store and was unprepared to see Valentine behind the counter dealing with customers. Immediately, he could see a difference in her. This wasn't the same shy girl from the hills he'd left behind.

Willheim looked at her, really studied her, and she was a beautiful sight to behold. His stomach dipped with the reality he was in love with this woman he had married. Maybe this separation was turning out to be a good thing, or at least it was for him.

She turned back from putting change into the oak cash drawer when she saw him. Without smiling, she ran her hands over her hair to smooth it. She turned to ask Savannah's boy, Sam, if he could handle things for a little while without her.

Will's grin was replaced by a more somber look as he realized Valen wasn't smiling. He suddenly cared whether she was glad to see him or not. Hat in hand, he followed her lead into the stockroom behind the privacy of a partition.

Facing each other, one seemed as hesitant as the other. Willheim finally broke the tension between them.

"Val, ya look good, Hon', real good. Are ya feelin' alright, with tha baby 'n' all, I mean?

"I was wrong ta have left ya alone for sa long."

As his eyes traced down from her face and back up again, the ample mound growing at her waist was obvious. It made him feel both embarrassed and uneasy at the same time. He'd had a sudden strong impulse to engulf her with his protection and confess he never should have left her alone for so long. The urge to reach out and stroke her face and lay a hand on the roundness of her belly was overpowering. Somehow, he didn't feel she'd welcome him doing either one.

"Yes, you were. I've not known what I should think. You've been gone from here for a long piece of time. I had about decided something happened to you, or maybe you didn't intend to ever come back at all."

Things were strained. The friction between them was uncomfortable. This sure wasn't the way Will had thought it would be today.

Unintentionally making it worse, he reached into his shirt pocket and pulled out the money she'd given him the day before he left. He handed the bills back to her, and she just stared at them.

Clumsily he said, "I, I, didn't use yer money. I brought only wild mustangs home instead a buying any stock. I'm anxious for ya to see 'em, Val. If you'd been at home when I came in from tha trail, ya would've seen 'em already."

He grimaced, realizing his words sounded like he was accusing. It was not how he'd meant them to be.

Valentine tucked in her bottom lip for a moment biting into it. She managed to control her voice when she asked with more gumption than he'd expected to hear from her.

"And where is my home exactly, Will? I couldn't think of any reason I had to stay where you left me. When Savannah Grace asked me to come and help her, I was glad to get away from there.

"So, here I am---and now here you are too. You're just today coming to see if I'm okay---even when you got back, you didn't bother yourself to come here and see me, mmmm. What am I supposed to think?

"Well, I'm staying on to work the store and not going back to the farm. Savannah can spend more time with the baby, and I'm wanted here.

"I take it this money means I'm not to be a part of the ranch. Well, you may not want me, Will, but I've found my own purposefulness. I'm happy here, and I'm needed."

Val looked down at the floor. She had talked to her husband so boldly. He reached out and lifted her chin upward, pinching it lightly with his thumb and index finger.

"Well, tha thing is ya don't really live here, Valentine. I've come ta take ya home with me where ya belong. It don't look right fer ya to be in town since I'm back. People are gonna talk."

He glanced down pointedly at her swelling belly again.

"Finish up what yer doin' in tha store 'n' get yer things together. I'm goin' in and talk ta Savannah and see my new nephew. Then I'll take ya back ta tha homeplace, where ya belong."

Willheim walked off angrier at himself than at her. He

knew this talk with Valentine hadn't gone well. He felt ashamed and wished he could suck the clipped words back into his mouth. Dog-gone-it, he hadn't expected her attitude!

He'd never seen or heard her act so quarrelsome before. It had hit him broadsided, but he couldn't keep from thinking she had a right to be cool. He should have found more gentle words to say.

Clearly, Valentine was beyond hurt by his extended absence. She was obviously not prepared to see him today. When he dictated, he was taking her home, unshed tears had collected in her eyes and glistened. There was nothing to be done about it now but to proceed, in for a penny, in for a pound!

Will was temporarily distracted by baby Seth. He was a tiny creature from head to toe. His large, roughened cowboy hands seemed like big, cumbersome bear paws, as he tried to juggle the infant. It was hard to believe he'd soon be a father himself when he was having such a hard time being a husband.

He peppered his sister with questions about Valentine and the baby she was carrying. "How long will it be until Val's time? Do you think she's doing alright? Is there anything she needs? Will it be awfully painful when the baby is born? How do you know they'll both be alright?"

By the time he finished rapidly firing questions, he was fairly distraught with worry and handed Seth back to his mother.

"Slow down Willheim! For being around livestock your whole life, you haven't learned much about nature. People and animals aren't very different. Females of every kind have been birthing their babies since the beginning of time.

"Yes, she'll have a hard time of it, but everything will happen when it happens. There's no stopping the inevitable, but most mothers and babies make it through the ordeal of birthing just fine.

"The main thing Valentine needs is you, Will! I take by all these questions you've decided you want this little ready-made family. I figured you'd come around, but I'm not so sure Valentine hasn't given up on you. You're going to prove you want her and the baby and show you feel this way for the right reasons.

"Valen will deliver this child sometime in August, probably. You two should be settled in together by then. She's a real sweetheart of a girl, Will. Make every effort to show her your heart is in the right place. You inherited yourself a good wife and got a well-bred baby in the bargain!"

Will pulled the stub of a pencil and a tattered list out of his shirt pocket.

"I'm building a house for us, but I don't want Val ta know yet 'cause it's a surprise. The carpenters are ready to start. It'll be finished in plenty of time.

"Savannah, I don't know a lot about lovin' a woman, but I'll learn. I'm happy to be a husband and a papa for Tavy's baby.

"Here's a list I made. Could you and Ely order me a real nice cookstove for her?"

"Of course, Will, but you may be the one in for a big surprise. While you've been out wandering all over the countryside, Val has been here improving herself and is more independent than when you left."

"Yeah, when we talked, I was taken aback by how she stood up for herself. You know, I kind of like the change, Savannah. She stood her ground."

"Both Meta and I have been watching her spirit grow gradually. While you've been off gallivanting, Valentine has been adapting to life here and educating herself. She's smart.

She can get a job before long if she wants and go anywhere, she pleases. You'd better hurry and make sure it's you she wants."

"I'm on it, Savannah. I do want Val to be with me. I'll build her the best home to live in!"

"Hurry it up, Willheim. The clock's ticking, Cowboy!"

Chapter 35

Thank You, God!

~Valentine

Valentine fretted silently riding back to the farm in the buggy. The last thing she had wanted was to leave the security of Savannah's family. Before she left, she pinned a note to Ella's pillow to find when she got home from school. Ella was the only real friend she'd ever made. Val was going to be alone without her.

Will had put her satchel in the back seat of the buggy along with a bundle Savannah had packed for her to take. Inside, she'd put piece goods, flannels, ribbons, and things to make baby clothes, diapers, bibs, and blankets.

Valentine kept her face turned from Will and pulled her bonnet low to hide the quiet tears. Will climbed in beside her and took up the reins. Once they were out of town, he laid his hand upon her knee, and promised, "I'm gonna take care a everything and make ya happy. You'll see Val, just give me a little more time."

No sooner had he settled back into his papa's house

with Meta Anna than he took off again. He had talked to his papa and sister behind closed doors, leaving her out of his life once more. Then he told her, "Goodbye," and kissed her on the cheek before he left.

Nothing seemed any different than before. Val hadn't counted on it anyway.

For the next few weeks, Valentine occupied herself with the contents of the bundle from Benton's store. She had watched Savannah making little things for her Baby Seth and had yearned to make some for her own baby. She industriously worked through the first of summer's heat radiating from the sun. When she was unsure how something should be done Meta patiently showed her.

Sometimes her sister-in-law would make lemonade and sit with her in the shade to enjoy the sweet drink. The two cut flannel into squares for diapers. They folded them and stacked them neatly ready for the baby.

Valen had a green thumb and enjoyed seeing things grow. She diligently helped Meta harvest vegetables and tend the garden in the early mornings or in the evenings when it wasn't so hot. Together, they canned and dried produce, braided onions to hang, and stocked the cool cellar under the farmhouse with food.

The fruits from the small orchard and the vegetables would feed the Brandts all through the winter. In a few more weeks, the men would butcher beef and pork. Some of it would be hung in the smokehouse and smoked. Other pieces were dried or packed in salt. Valentine had never thought she'd see so much food.

Martin Brandt sat on the porch with his daughter-in-law after supper. The old man puffed on his pipe and chewed the stem while she embroidered delicate edges around soft, flannel blankets. Val and Papa Martin had conversations and formed a very comfortable bond.

She was growing larger and more cumbersome by the day. She relished the feel of the baby's movements and thought of Tavias. Valentine tried not to think about what Willheim might be doing.

He came to see her two or three times a week and asked her if she needed anything. She didn't want anything at Meta house because there was always plenty, and Papa and Meta's family were good to her. What she wanted was Willheim to be her husband, but she never said it out loud.

When he came, he was usually unkept, tired to the bone, and too weary to stay for long. She came to expect little support from him. Sometimes she even went to bed before he left. Val quit showing him her handwork or talking about the garden and how the cellar was bulging with foodstuffs.

By the middle of July, the yellow haired girl felt heavy, swollen, and ugly. No wonder Willheim found her lacking. She couldn't stand herself either and didn't blame him for keeping his distance. In fact, she even quit caring what he thought.

At night, she'd fall into bed not long after supper burdened by sadness, loneliness, weariness, and the extra burden of weight she was carrying. She often fell into despair and would cry herself to sleep.

This deep depression did not go unnoticed by Meta Anna, and she sent a note to her brother putting her foot down. She told her brother to come immediately and get his wife before she melted clean away from despair. The house cannot be kept a secret from Val any longer.

~*Will*

So, he came after dark, and Nick helped him load the wagon with the very cradle he and Tavy had lain in once upon a time. He stole Valentine's wedding quilt, the things she'd made for the baby, and other things Meta had boxed for him to stock the kitchen.

He worked with one of his hands to make Valentine's new home a welcoming place before shutting the door and going to bed for the last time in the bunkhouse with his hands. Tomorrow, he would bring his bride here to woo and court her in private in this special place he'd prepared for her. He loved Valentine, and it felt good to be bringing her to their home.

In the middle of the morning, he bathed and cleaned up taking extra care to impress her. He took one more walk through the house before he left on Rope Tail. He'd bring Val back in the farm buggy with Rope Tail tied to the back. He felt prideful everything in the house was fresh, bright, and cheerful. The kitchen and root cellar were well stocked to the brim.

The sun had slipped behind the clouds making the sky overcast. The air had turned unusually cool all of a sudden. The westward breeze picked up steadily, and the smell of rain coming was strong. Lightning sparkled off and on in the distance followed by the sounds of rumbling thunder.

When he arrived at Papa's house, he was met by a frantic Meta Anna coming down the staircase. In her hand, she held a note Valentine had written and left on her empty bed.

You are so kind. Thank you.

Will doesn't want me. I must find a place

of my own before the baby gets here.

You can send my things later. Please tell my friend,

Ella, goodbye for me.

Valentine

An intense crack of light shown through the window glass followed by a deafening clap of thunder. Alarm registered on every face. A downpour hit the ground in sheets causing noise with its force.

Willheim couldn't hide the torment gutting him. The joy of his perfect surprise was washed away and forgotten. The most important thing was to find his Valentine, not Tavy's but his!

"When did she leave?" he yelled over the increasing noise of the storm.

Meta Anna cried, "I have no idea. I found this note on her pillow just now!"

Nick ran in ignoring the water he was dripping on the floor.

"Little Dove is gone from the stall along with her tack. I fed her grain only a little while ago. Where's Val? Surely, she's not somewhere out in this storm! It's bad out there."

Willheim yelled, "I'm going after her."

He and Nick ran down the slippery porch steps to get their horses saddled. Will took off at a gallop. Nick would follow as soon as he could.

If anything happened to Valentine and the baby, it was his fault, and he knew it! He didn't think he could live with the guilt. Visions of another storm when Adam got hurt in the stampede and died long ago played through his mind. He couldn't let the storm win and take another person from him.

Both Meta and Susannah had tried to warn him to give Valen more attention, but he had not heeded their advice. He had been working so hard to make a home for her, and he was still hurting from losing Tavy. His selfishness had cost him Val. It was precious time wasted on himself, while leaving the woman he loved and married alone.

He pushed his horse like a madman through the driving rain with his dogs keeping up with them. Rope Tail gave Will everything he had like always. He ran like the wind with the rain pounding them both, the lightning striking, and the thunder banging.

The dogs started barking above the noise and ran off to the right, away from the road. Will saw Little Dove standing riderless, back bowed against the rain with saddle slipped to one side. The dogs ran past the gray mare in the tall, wet grass and got to Val first. They had led Will to her.

He vaulted from his heaving horse in one giant leap

and made it to his girl's side. He knelt and sheltered her head with his hat and wiped the rain from her face with his wet bandana. It was all he had. Her eyes fluttered as he called her name over and over with tears and rain mixed streaming down his own face.

Unconsolable, he cried out, "Val, Val, Val—wake up---please don't be hurt---open yer eyes, Darlin'---say somethin' to me---please say somethin'---I'm in love with ya, Valentine, don't leave me now---you can't---ya gist can't! I want ya with me, Girl! I love you 'n' our baby! Please, be alright, Honey!

Her eyes opened, and she looked up into his face. "Do ya, Will, do ya really love me? Can---can I be yer wife now, truly be yer wife?"

She reached her hand up to touch his jaw but couldn't quite reach it before it fell away from weakness. Darkness enveloped her again, but she was breathing!

Will reared his head back and hollered, "Jesus, help me to get her back to Meta Anna!"

This is when Nick reached them.

Chapter 36

Let's Get Something Straight!

~Willheim Brandt

Little Dove's cinch had loosened, allowing the saddle to slip sideways, and she'd been thrown from her horse. Hitting the ground and lying unconscious in the cold wind and under the relentless downpour of the storm had taken a toll on her body.

Nick had frantically ridden for the doctor after handing her up to Will who headed for Papa's house as fast as Rope Tail could take them. Will knew he needed to get Valentine out of her wet clothes and then get her warm as soon as possible.

When the doctor came, he was immediately concerned about the quick onset of congestion he could hear in her chest. Every breath she took sounded labored. After such prolonged exposure to the elements, pneumonia could set up quickly.

After examining Valen, he could see she had a concussion where she'd hit her head on a rock. The wound needed stitches. Her left forearm was swollen, but the bone wasn't broken. The baby wasn't moving, but there was an encouraging heartbeat. The chance of delivering early was a risk.

The next days would be critical. Willheim sat beside Valentine's bed praying for forty-eight hours. Val would need bed rest until the doctor was sure the danger had passed. He prescribed a foul-smelling plaster to be reapplied to her chest every two hours in an effort to clear the congestion from her lungs.

He told Meta to make strong willow bark tea to relieve headaches and the fever she was already running. Nick killed a chicken for Meta to stew a clear broth for nourishment.

Meta offered multiple times to share turns sitting with Val, but Will refused to leave her side. He sat in a chair and held vigil over his wife, nodding off occasionally with his head on her bed. Willheim placed all the blame for this accident on himself.

If he had just shared his own pain and grief over Tavy's death with her, he could have explained why he had to stay so busy. Instead, he'd stayed silent, pushing her away. If he'd just told her about the house he was building, it would have given her hope for their future together.

Will should have told her how much he loved her before now. If he had just been open with his feelings, Val and the baby wouldn't be in danger today, and his heart wouldn't feel like it was going to shatter into pieces.

The first time he laid eyes on Tavy's Valentine; Will had known he was going to fall in love with her. What man could not?

He was just too pig-headed to admit the truth to himself. The fact she rightfully belonged to his brother made him feel guilty to claim her. He felt like an interloper on the outside looking in.

God, forgive me please and let my little family live.

Give me another chance to be the good husband Valentine deserves and a good father for our baby. Please, Lord.

In the hours since the accident, Valentine had slept restlessly and woke confused and bewildered at irregular intervals. She was barely lucid enough to take spoons of willow bark tea, water, and broth, but his sister kept offering it to her. Meta Anna took advantage of these times to attend to her personal needs while Will took a break.

Thank goodness the congestion had begun to break up, and she was coughing productively. On the third afternoon Valentine woke fatigued but more clear-headed than she had been. When she went back to sleep, Will climbed into bed and threw an arm over her. It was the first time he'd ever slept with her. His unshaven face was so close, warm puffs of his breath reached her neck.

~*Valentine*

She lay very still trying to make sense of it all and regain her bearings. Something had definitely changed between them, and she sorted through thoughts trying to define what and when it happened. She fought hard to remember.

Thunder, lightning, her horse running, the saddle twisting, falling, and, and, and---Will was there! Willheim was there! He loved me. Loved me? He loves me!

She stirred and one hand automatically reached for her baby making sure it was alright. At the movement of her hand, Will woke with a jerk of his body and raised upon his elbow smiling down at her.

Then his lips lowered to kiss her, slowly and softly at first, afraid Valentine might refuse him. She didn't shy away, so he deepened the kiss. Then, they both smiled and kissed again and again before he pulled back and looked down at her with a stern face.

"What did ya think ya were doin' ridin' out in a storm?

Ya could a gotten yerself 'n' tha baby killed. Don't ya ever do somethin' sa foolish again, Val. My heart can't take it!

"We need ta get a few important things straight right now, Honey. From now on, we're gonna talk our problems out 'n' never, never run from each other again. Ya got it. I'll start tellin' ya everything on my mind, 'n' you better do tha same."

Chapter 37

Little Fawn Ella

~*Willheim*

As soon as it was safe for Val to travel, Will wasted no time loading her into the buggy and taking her home, their real home. Her house was ready and waiting for her to claim it. It was no longer a secret and never should have been in the first place. He had been a fool to keep his thoughts and plans to himself. He'd been wrong to wedge distance between them for so long

If Val had known about the house before the first nail was pounded it might have given her a view of the bright future she so desperately needed to see on the horizon. What Will wouldn't give to have skipped the near deadly consequences of Val's escapade! The fear of it had brought him abruptly to his senses.

Obviously, he had not been dealing well with Tavias's death for months. The acute pain of grief caused by the loss of his closest brother and family anchor had caused him to act irrationally and selfishly.

Only the scare of almost losing Val and the baby had

opened his eyes and heart completely. Now, the reality of neglecting Valentine to suffer alone shamed him, but he'd make amends.

This morning was a bright new day for them both. He couldn't wait to show her the house he'd built where they would live and raise a family. It had a long porch for sitting like the one where he'd grown up. He could just imagine it being filled with children laughing and playing.

The house he'd built for his Valentine was so much more than just a structure made for shelter. This ranch house was the place they'd settle into a lifetime spent together. Every nail and board had been laid and pounded with love forming an unbreakable commitment. It was evidence, without question, he and his bride were finally home.

They would be glued together by Tavey's seed and Willheim's seed forever-forward.

Their story and the stories of their heirs to come might be written down on pages worthy enough to be bound into volumes. Who, but God, knew the future and what the next twenty-five years held in store for Will and Val. No writer, even one with the wildest of imaginations, could make up the events and circumstances bringing them to even this historic day in time!

Valentine wrapped her arms tightly around her husband's neck as he scooped her off the buggy seat and carried her across the threshold. He sat her feet down on the spacious parlor floor and watched her face intently. Her eyes sparkled as she turned herself in a circle to take in the large fireplace, the windows, the bookshelves, furnishings, and every little detail.

"Val, you see there aren't curtains, 'cause I want ya ta pick out tha calicos 'n' colors ya want. I was thinkin' ya might like ta make 'em yerself."

Her big smile and bouncing chin told him he'd guessed right!

Cupping her elbow, he guided her into the kitchen, and she walked immediately to the blue, fancy cast iron stove next to a cooking counter with a recessed sink. There was a small kitchen pump for water. An inside door led to a washroom with a big copper tub. The shelves were stocked with towels and bars of soap smelling like roses.

The other door in the kitchen opened into a mudroom for washing up after working outside, hanging coats and hats, and to leave muddy boots and the like. It also had a second door opening out onto a back stoop with two steps leading to the well and a full-sized outside pump. The clothesline was standing ready for use.

The outhouse was a polite ways from the house. It was a colorful sight with a brightly decorated door and a steep shingled roof matching the one on the house. Between there and the barn was the chicken coop.

"Chickens will be delivered as soon as I tell tha man who sells 'em. It won't be long 'fore ya have all tha eggs ya can use 'n' baby chicks runnin' around. We can have fried chicken too!

There's the smokehouse, and the food cellar is under the mudroom, so ya don't even have ta go outside in tha winter ta get what ya need.

"To start, I only had two bedrooms built, but we can add more later as our family grows."

The two bedrooms were large and furnished with new and handmade furniture in addition to a few pieces from Papa's attic. A four-poster bed for Val and Will to share was in the largest room, and two sizable, braided rugs were on each side of the bed. The bed was neatly made and topped with Val's patchwork wedding quilt she brought with her from the hills.

At the foot of the bed was an old wooden immigrant's chest. It had carried one of the families' possessions across the water to the promise land of America. Now it holds all of the fresh baby things Valentine had made for the baby.

The old wooden cradle where both Tavy and Will had lain as well as Matilda's and Martin's other babies was waiting in the second bedroom. The cradle had been well-crafted by Martin Brandt's own young hands.

In a couple of weeks, Ely drove Ella out to stay with Valen until after the baby came. The girl took over the kitchen, washing, cleaning, and doing heavy chores. She moved into the room where the cradle sat. Her presence allowed Will to return to ranch work for full days again.

Life on the horse ranch fell into an easy rhythm until the peace was broken early one afternoon. Ella dashed out to fetch Uncle Will from the corral where he was working a green broke mustang. Hearing her words, he yelled at one of the hands to go into Sweetwater for the doctor.

Will didn't stop to think or change horses. Instead, he rode the green broke mustang right out of the gate with his dogs following and raced to alert Meta Anna. He saw Ely working in a field before he made it to the house and yelled at him.

"Send Meta, it's Val's time! Hurry!"

As soon as Ely waved his hat in an answer to let him know he understood, Willheim was already turning the horse to take off the same direction from which they'd just come.

The mare he rode was good and truly broken after the paces he'd demanded of her this day. An old granny could ride her to the church picnic balancing a couple of pies.

By the time he made it back to the corral and handed the mare off to a hand, he headed off toward the house in a dead run. He stopped short at the outside pump just long enough to shower his head with cold water, wash his hands with a bar of white soap, and swallow at least a quart of water.

He rushed up the steps, slamming the screen door on his way into the kitchen. He came to an abrupt stop when he slid into his niece.

"Why are ya in here moppin' the floor, Ella? Shouldn't ya be in there with Val? You can do tha housework later!"

Ella stood up resting a hand on her hip and countered, "Uncle Will, I have been with Aunt Val a good while and have her settled into the bed. She's okay for right now, and we're just waiting. I came back in here to mop up the floor where her water broke. She was mixing up a batch of biscuits when it happened."

It was doubtful he heard about the biscuits. He was already outside the bedroom door by then.

Later, when the sun had gone down, the ranch's cowboys along with Wild Ned were sitting with Willheim, Papa, Ely, Morgan, Mateas, and Nick outside the bunkhouse trying to keep him from fidgeting and worrying about the ordeal of birthing progressing inside the house.

They passed around a bottle of Red Eye, one of the hands played a guitar and another had a mouth organ. They were singing, talking loudly, telling stories, and laughing. This racket was to keep the nervous father from hearing noises which might pierce him to the limits of his very soul.

Meta, Savannah, and baby Seth were inside with Val along with the doctor. Ella was in charge of the older children. They were sitting under a tree playing games and telling their own stories. The brush dogs were smart, and they'd bedded down in the barn already.

By the time Savannah Grace walked out to the bunkhouse, Will was well on his way to being three sheets to the wind!

She announced, "Valentine has given Willheim and this family a fine, pretty baby girl who looks like her mama. Mother and child are doing fine.

"Val is asking for you, brother, but mind yourself, your gals are awfully tired. Don't be scared by how peaky your wife looks. Her feathers will fluff out again by this time tomorrow. Bringing a baby into the world is hard work."

At the bedroom door, he took off his hat. He had

215

sobered up quite a bit just on the way from the bunkhouse because of the seriousness of the situation. When he caught sight of a pale Valentine resting on the bed, it sobered him the rest of the way.

Meta had cleaned the bed, helped her change into a fresh nightgown, combed her damp hair, and tied it back with a bright pink ribbon. It didn't hide the weariness reflected in her face. Looking down at her baby, Will thought his wife was the most beautiful sight he'd ever seen.

At first, Valentine didn't see him standing at the door taking the scene all in. Once she did, a smile touched her lips, and he tossed his hat on the floor under the cradle. He'd moved it into their room earlier. Will stepped forward and bent to kiss Val on the forehead.

The tiny babe's rosebud mouth formed a ring attached to her mama's nipple as she rested against a soft, fleshy breast. He was amazed at how earnestly she was sucking. He reached out a rough hand used to hard work and caressed her little ball of a head covered in a few, sparse curls.

"Will, I need you to help me put her on the other side now."

"Oh, Val, I don't want a hurt ya none. What do ya want me ta do? Just tell me."

"She won't break, and neither will I."

He watched, fascinated as Val inserted the tip of a finger into one tiny corner of the baby's mouth, breaking the suction. The release made a little pop surprising him and causing him to laugh quietly.

"Now, pick her up, support her neck, and shift her to the other breast."

Clearly the babe hadn't finished eating, and she started the most pitiful whimpering, making him carefully hurry with this delicate task. As soon as Val and the baby were repositioned, Valentine offered her the fresh nipple. The baby eagerly latched onto it, making a couple of smacking noises until she settled. White translucent bubbles escaped along the edge of the seal for a moment before everyone stilled.

"Prop me up some, Will. I need to sit up more."

He braced her shoulders, lifting her forward just enough to wedge an extra feather pillow into place. He was being so careful not to cause Valentine physical stress. He felt like he was handling a China doll.

"Thank you. That feels so much better."

He moved to sit gingerly on the bed by his wife's shoulder. Reaching out a hand, he stroked her sweat dampened hair and then caressed her cheek.

She smiled weakly and proudly up at her babe's pa, and asked him, "Isn't she pretty, Will? Isn't she perfect in every way? Have you ever seen the like? She's so soft and sweet just like a little fawn."

"She's a beauty a'right, jus' like her mama."

"Can we name her Fawn, Will, Fawn Ella?"

"It sounds like a nice name ta me---Fawn Ella Brandt. He leaned in closer and kissed Valentine on the lips.

"Ya need ta sleep, Darlin'. Ya look all tuckered out."

Meta came back into the room and handed little Fawn over to her Pa. He cradled the child in his large hands as delicately as if he was holding onto a sack of eggs. He softly kissed the baby's cheek and welcomed her into the world. Right then and there he made a solemn vow.

I vow I'll never let anything or anyone drive a wedge between Valentine and me again, and I won't ever allow anyone to hurt Fawn Ella or any child of mine as long as I'm alive---so help me, God.

An unselfish vow made by a good and Godly person is usually based on morally good intentions, meant for the sole benefit of other people. Unselfish, good, and Godly are words certainly applying to Willheim Brandt.

What could possibly go wrong?

Chapter 38

The Forgotten Cameo

~Elizabeth Hartley a Few Months Ago

Elizabeth Hartley fell into a dark, clinical depression after the cold rejection of her pawn, Willheim Brandt. She had great plans of eventually leaving The House of Satin in fine style riding on his coat-tails. She had counted on the cowboy to be her ticket to the respectable life she had always dreamed of living.

Lizzy had invested a lot of time grooming him to always come back to her. She assumed she could reel him in like a fish when she was ready to leave here. She was the one using him, not the other way around. How dare he continue coming back to her bed for years only to abruptly walk away one day!

He disappeared as if she had never existed? Her vindictive nature was never going to allow Willheim Brandt to desert her without retribution. Hell, hath no fury as a woman scorned! A hate-filled grudge boiled inside of her soul. Elizabeth Hartley would not stop until she exacted her revenge no matter how long it took. Someday she would destroy him, and he'd never see it coming.

In her mind, she had mulled over and over, again and again, every detail of what she remembered from the afternoon he had walked out on her. He had come to The Satin with all sweetness and a costly gift. She had not suspected anything was amiss. He brought an exquisite cameo encased in gold, and she had worn it around her neck ever since.

She was blindsided to find out why he'd really come. He just wanted one last romp in the hay before he said goodbye. Her recollections always ended with unparalleled rage and the vow he would pay dearly for his rejection. If it was the last thing she ever did on this side of the grass, she'd make him sorry.

Elizabeth's own time of giving birth was not far off on the calendar. The unborn fetus within her rolled and moved, jabbing and crowding her insides until she was as nervous as a cat! Her midsection was swollen and stretched like a cow. She was uncomfortable in bed and out of it. Her feet no longer fit into her shoes!

She took her hostility out on Nadine and her handmaid, Mavis. They were the only two people ever allowed to see her since the afternoon Will abandoned her. She made insulting comments and unreasonable demands of them. It made it difficult for them to take care of her.

In the beginning, the only other person in the world who knew she was pregnant was Dr. Matthews, and Elizabeth had threatened the doctor to keep him quiet. She didn't want Nadine to find out until it was too late for Will's baby to be aborted.

Elizabeth truly hated Willheim who'd gotten her into this mess, and she hated this baby but thought it might possibly come in handy someday to use against the cowboy! She cursed both the father and the child daily. She missed the glamorous, bodacious life she'd once enjoyed as a high-priced whore in the elite House of Satin.

On this particular night there was a full moon. In the Satin, the noises coming from all over the house were particularly loud and raunchy. No one took notice of the occasional screams coming from Nadine's private quarters where Elizabeth lay and bucked in the throes of labor. Her noises could not be distinguished from any others heard around the house.

In labor she held tightly in one hand a red velvet bag secured by a black satin ribbon. Nine months ago, Will dropped it between her delicate, naked breasts.

He had said, "Here you go, Liz. This is for you. It's pretty like you are."

She grabbed it and pulled one end of the ribbon releasing the opening of the sack. She emptied its contents into the cup of her palm.

An exquisite cameo of the rarest beauty, framed in gold, and hanging from a chain spilled out. An elegant woman's cream-colored image was carved on the canvas of a cameo shell. The image shone brightly against a rich, caramel-colored background. It instantly became her greatest treasure in the world.

Tonight, relief came at last when a baby boy gushed forth from her loins in a stream of frothy, bloody liquid, and drained the last bit of strength Lizzy had left. So severe were the rigors of birthing, the doctor administered morphine to ease the pain and a larger enough dose to make her pass out.

He stitched together the large, irregular tears as best he could. Then, he told Nadine the girl would never be able to conceive another child.

Her recovery was slow. She refused to see the baby but insisted he be named Billy Hart. She refused to let him nurse. Mavis kept him alive with a goatmilk concoction her mammy had taught her to make during the days of slavery.

Little Billy Hart thrived under Mavis's nursing and

Nadine's coddling. In spite of his mother's hate, he was a happy baby who would grow into a strong young man in the years ahead.

His evil mother would figure out a way to use Billy Hart in a dastardly scenario against his father. She would deal him the most devastating blow imaginable. It would be vengeance by blood.

Epilogue

Through the Years

A fire fueling by the desire for retribution usually burns down with time. In the vicious reasoning of a scorned woman, however, hate can smolder until unthinkable punishment is served. No matter how long it takes, Elizabeth Hartley will have her shocking revenge.

Elizabeth is truly a sinister enemy, a black widow waiting for years to stick a knife into the soul of Willheim Brandt. The weapons she chooses are his own son, Billy Hart, and his own daughter, Fawn Ella.

Billy doesn't know who his father is, but he inherently follows in his footsteps and becomes quite the cowboy with a horse ranch of his own in East Texas. At the same time, Fawn Ella knows and adores her papa, Willheim Brandt, and her sweet Mama, Valentine.

What will happen when Elizabeth Hartley's evil deeds set these two siblings fathered by the same man on a collision course once the time is perfect?

The Cameo Trail has just begun in Book 1, titled Willheim Brandt. The trail's ultimate climax ends in Book 2, titled Billy Hart. Each can be read as a standalone.

ABOUT THE AUTHOR

Jana Dahmen is from Sweetwater, Texas. She understands the emotional highs and lows of the spirit and the physical exhaustion associated with ranching and farming in big sky country. Nothing is ever easy there, but the rewards of using two hands and a faith in God to make the land produce are great.

She was born and raised on the grass plains of West Texas with endless wind, dust, and desert conditions. Rain was always welcomed and an occasion worthy of rejoicing. To a child of the west, the glorious rainbows following a rainstorm stretched from end to end across the sky. The bright colored arches were a spectacular sight.

She has never forgotten the people and characters she knew and observed personally in West Texas. Every cowboy, field hand, rancher, farmer, landowner, country wife, and child are worthy to have their stories told.

Her historical fiction books are based in the 1800's when America was just getting settled and going through the growing pains of new beginnings. Each volume reflects glimpses into the past woven among the perceptions and depths of the story's characters written between the pages.

Today, Jana lives in Wichita, Kansas, another old west

cowboy town, in a farmhouse built in 1890. She feels right at home here with her artist husband, a spoiled Boston Terrier, and her memories.